"Will you please shut up and listen to me?"

To Kelly's surprise, Grey did stop insulting her long enough to listen to an explanation.

"I am not, as you so crudely put it, shacked up with Marcel," she continued. "I'm Kelly Barnes, and I'm in charge of this camp while dad's sick."

"You're a pretty good actress," Grey drawled, "but you don't seem to know that Barnes's daughter is a grown woman, not a high-school rabble-rouser."

Kelly took a deep breath. "Mr. Scofield, I am a fully qualified caterer, a cordon bleu chef, and twenty-four years old. Would you like to see my passport or my driver's license? Or, since you've had dinner, maybe you will consider believing the truth. Otherwise, that was the last meal you'll eat here until I get an apology!"

Wolf
at the Door

by

VICTORIA GORDON

Harlequin Books

TORONTO • LONDON • LOS ANGELES • AMSTERDAM
SYDNEY • HAMBURG • PARIS • STOCKHOLM • ATHENS • TOKYO

Original hardcover edition published in 1981
by Mills & Boon Limited

ISBN 0-373-02433-9

Harlequin edition published October 1981

CHAPTER ONE

KELLY BARNES stood at the rear of the school auditorium, idly wishing as she sometimes did that she hadn't ceased growing at five foot three. At times like this, her slight, small stature was a distinct nuisance, and one that grew worse as more and more people crowded in around her. She could no longer see the stage or the speakers with their huge maps and diagrams, and the growing rumble of discontented voices around her made it increasingly difficult even to hear.

All she could see, in fact, was a jumble of bush shirts and blue jeans that seemed to be the uniform of the scruffy crowd of students around her. They were all bigger than Kelly, and she was mildly disconcerted that most looked older as well, although none of them were anywhere near her own twenty-four years, she thought. Her small size, long, wavy carrot-coloured hair and masses of freckles all contributed to make Kelly look about seventeen, no matter how often she strove never to act that age.

As the restlessness of the crowd intensified, she gave up all hope of following the address from the stage, and began shifting her way through the massed bodies in a bid to reach the foyer and gain breathing space. She was nearly at the exit when the first egg was thrown, and the next few moments passed in a horrifying blur of frightening panic.

Hemmed in by the angry, chanting students with their barrage of missiles, Kelly lost all interest in the Kakwa Wilderness she had come to learn about. Her only interest was in getting out of that room with its building potential for violence. She struggled against the throng, cursing her small size even more than usual as she kicked at shins and stamped on insteps in her desperation to fight clear of the mob. She heard only dimly the banshee wail of the approaching police sirens, but the mob of protesters had also heard, and the students' reaction was quicker than her own.

Wheeling with unexpected precision, the mob bolted for the exits, carrying Kelly along like a water-borne leaf. Someone thrust a bundle of leaflets into her hands as they passed, only seconds before somebody else rammed her in the back, throwing her forward and down beneath the trampling boots of the fleeing students.

Kelly curled instinctively as she struck the floor, but her fear-widened eyes squeezed shut defensively at the sight of what seemed like hundreds of stampeding feet. Her scream of terror was lost in the cries of the mob, and as the first foot struck her she clenched her hands convulsively on both her handbag strap and the leaflets she still held. She felt the pain of that first kick, but the next one awaited by her shuddering body never arrived. Instead, she was plucked from the parquet floor by a pair of huge hands that held her with a curiously gentle firmness as their owner fought through the tide of human panic towards the doorway.

Kelly was flung across her rescuer's shoulder like a sack of meal, and she opened her eyes to find with some amazement that she was looking *down* at the surging throng of frantic students that divided around her position like water around a rock. Beneath her stomach she could feel the flex of powerful muscles as her rescuer fought to keep his balance in the press, and the arm around her middle was rigid as an iron bar.

Still, they made progress, and after a minute that seemed to take forever, Kelly and her steed turned out of the crowd and into the relative open of the foyer. It was then, with a pair of hands firm at her waist as she was hoisted from the man's shoulder, that she got her first look at him.

Grey hair, not steel-grey but a silver still laced with

traces of black, curled thickly above a square-cut, handsome, sun-burned face. The hair was misleading; meeting his eyes from only inches away as the man held Kelly before setting her on her feet, she could see that he was not old, but prematurely grey. He was still in his thirties, she guessed, before her brown eyes locked with a pair of icy grey ones that froze her with their intensity.

As her feet touched the floor, she had to look up quite severely to maintain contact with those eyes, and she was struck by the pale anger that blazed from them.

'Thank you,' she whispered, ashamed immediately of her hesitant whisper, but unable to command any more force into her voice.

Her tremulous smile had no effect on the sternly handsome face above her, except perhaps to make it even more stern.

'Don't bother,' growled a voice that rasped with throaty anger. 'Just be glad you've got more luck than brains.'

The man's haughty anger and obvious contempt fired the temper that Kelly knew so well and usually managed to control, and with the fright she had just had, control was easier to think about than manage.

'Well pardon me,' she said with an angry shake of her head. 'If it was going to upset you so much to help me, I can't imagine why you bothered.'

'I hope it's because I'm a little more tolerant than that bunch of hoodlums you associate with,' he replied coldly, his eyes straying down to glare at the bundle of leaflets Kelly still had in her trembling fingers.

Her glance followed his, and she looked up to meet his eyes with abrupt surprise. 'Oh,' she said, 'but I . . .' She had intended to deny any association with the throng of angry students, but he gave her no chance at all.

'But nothing,' he said curtly, reaching out with one hand to wrench the leaflets from her hand and fling them on to an adjacent window ledge. 'Children like you give me a royal pain with your senseless violence and protests against things you know absolutely nothing about.'

Kelly tried again to interject, but he continued as if she hadn't opened her mouth, and his own anger seemed to grow with every word he uttered.

'You sit in some classroom on your saucy little butt and plot how to run the world, too stupid to realise you don't have the experience to run a bath for yourself,' he snarled. 'And *you're* probably worse than the rest; judging from that accent you haven't been in this country long enough to know which way is up, but you're just *so* ready to throw eggs and abuse at the people who work to develop the country so that maybe you'll have a job to go to when you're old enough . . .'

His gravelly voice continued its tirade, but Kelly lost the train of his remarks in her own battle to keep her temper. Around them, uniformed policemen were busily rounding up the unruly crowd of students, indifferent to the obscene shouts and taunts that heralded their task. But for Kelly it was as if she was alone in the world with this pale-eyed, angry man who seemed determined to vent his anger upon her. She was only vaguely aware of the approaching uniform until a new voice halted the man's assault.

'You saving this one for yourself, Grey? Or can we dump her in with the others?'

Kelly looked up at the tall policeman who approached them, instinctively moving toward him until an iron hand clamped on to her shoulder. She swung her head around to see her rescuer's curt nod of dismissal, then back to catch the policeman's wry expression as he turned away to join his colleagues.

Angered, Kelly twisted in a bid for freedom, but she was only pulled closer to the grey-eyed stranger whose voice rumbled in her ear.

'Stand still and shut up! You're too young to go to jail.'

The wisdom of the statement struck through Kelly's own

indignation. If this man thought she was one of the demonstrators, and certainly the policeman had thought so, jail seemed a very plausible possibility, she realised. And that shock, combined with her earlier fear of being trampled, struck shivers through her slender frame. Her knees turned to jelly and she reached up to brush ineffectually at the tears she felt gathering on her eyelashes. She stumbled slightly, and would have collapsed but for the firm hand that remained clamped about her shoulder.

The man called Grey didn't return to his verbal assault, and the two of them stood in silence as the police rounded up the last of the demonstrators and departed. Only when the last police vehicle had departed the school parking lot did the hand remove itself from Kelly's shoulder.

She turned to meet those harsh grey eyes once again, and despite her own anger at the misconception she faced, she managed to stammer out a second thanks. It was brusquely ignored.

'Just let it be a lesson to you,' the man said harshly. 'If I were you, I'd go back to England where you belong. It's obvious you're not going to fit in very damned well here.'

And before Kelly could muster the words to explain anything to him, he turned on his heel and strode away, leaving her alone in the school foyer with a burgeoning anger and nowhere to release it.

'You arrogant . . . insufferable . . . detestable . . . !' Her rage expanded beyond adjectives as she struggled with the unfamiliar gears of her father's large pick-up truck, cautiously wending her way through the crowded Grande Prairie streets towards the small house where Geoff Barnes lived when he was in town.

Throughout the drive, she composed haughty responses to the now-absent man who had so sternly reprimanded her in the mistaken belief that she was one of those ratbag students. He'd been right about one thing, and one thing only, and it had nothing to do with the rest of his assumptions, she decided. Kelly was, admittedly, a newcomer to Canada. She had been there only three days, in fact, and she had seen nothing of the country at all except two airports and portions of the north-western Alberta city of Grande Prairie.

Sneering as she glanced into the wide rear-view mirror, she wondered how he would react if he knew that she wasn't a student, at least not any more, but was actually a graduate catering economist and a Cordon Bleu chef in the bargain. Not to mention the fact that she had attended that night's meeting about the Kakwa Wilderness not to throw eggs or abuse, but to learn something about the area where she would be working for the next year or so.

She shook her head angrily. At least, she thought, she had been able to gain some information before the meeting degenerated into a small-scale riot. Just how significant that information would be, she didn't yet know.

But at least she now knew, from studying the maps and displays before the meeting had started, that the Kakwa Wilderness was nearly a hundred air miles south-west of Grande Prairie, near the northern limit of where the Rocky Mountains formed the Alberta–British Columbia border. The scenic highlight of the region was Kakwa Falls, a spectacular waterfall on the high Kakwa River, which flowed east and north to join first the Smoky and then the mighty Peace River as the mountain waters flowed north and east towards the high Arctic.

The region around the Kakwa was significant for more than scenery, however. The increased world-wide search for fossil fuels had brought increasing oil and gas exploration to the region, with Grande Prairie as a major supply centre. Also, there were immense coal deposits and timber resources, all open to eventual exploitation.

It was this search for resources that was responsible for Kelly's father's presence. He was a specialist, not in exploration, but in the service area that was linked to it. His camp catering operation provided the housing, food and amenities for a number of exploration and development teams in several locations throughout northern Alberta and British Columbia, although the small camp in the Kakwa region had significance far beyond its size.

The Kakwa camp was the first that Barnes Catering had provided for a massive consortium headed by a man named Scofield, and Geoff Barnes had made it his own personal project until a mysterious illness had landed him in Grande Prairie hospital only the day before Kelly's arrival from England.

His confinement, expected to last at least another month, had severely blighted his daughter's planned re-union with the father she had known only as an infrequent visitor to the home she shared in England with a mother who'd divorced Geoff Barnes when Kelly was still a baby. Mrs Barnes had been unable to cope with the isolation and the rigours of developing a then tiny catering concern in the rugged Canadian north country, but her bitterness and disillusionment hadn't thwarted Kelly's lifetime dream of joining her father in the business.

With his encouragement, she had studied extensively in both catering and cooking, and then spent some time both in England and on the Continent putting her studies to practical application, until she felt confident enough to take a full working role with her father in the business.

And when she reached home after the meeting, she suddenly realised it would be only two more days before she would have the involvement she had always wanted. She would be on her way to Kakwa camp to take full charge of the operation, replacing her father's second-in-command so that he could reassume supervision of the many other far-flung camps in the operation.

'I'm not all that happy at throwing you in at the deep end like this,' Geoff Barnes had told his daughter only that morning, 'but Marcel Leduc is needed to keep the other camps in order and there's no way I can return to Kakwa myself. If Marcel and Scofield got along better, I'd have second thoughts, but for some reason they don't, and that's a complication we can do without.'

During visiting times, Geoff Barnes had been able to explain to Kelly most of what she thought was needed to help her cope with the job, and he assured her that the expertise of Marcel Leduc would always be available in any event via the radio-phone network.

'But why don't he and this Scofield man get along?' she had asked with genuine concern. If maintaining Scofield's good will was so obviously important, she wanted to know what pitfalls that she herself must avoid.

'Too much alike in some ways, too different in others,' was the ambiguous reply. 'And nothing for you to worry your pretty head over. Scofield is one of the finest men I know, but he's inclined to be a bit overbearing at times, or maybe impatient is a better word. Anyway, I've never had problems with him and I see no reason for you to have any. Just flash those big brown eyes at him, if all else fails. He's not too old that a pretty girl like you won't have some advantages.'

'Just so long as *both* of you realise that I came here for a career,' Kelly had replied with a wry grin. 'And if that's a matchmaking gleam I see in your eyes, it's just as well you're going to be stuck in this hospital. I don't need those kind of problems on top of the ones I'll have.'

'You won't need my interference that way,' her father had assured her. 'The man–woman ratio is so far out of balance that you'll have to fight off the lads with a great big stick. Pretty girls are scarce up here, and brown-eyed redheads as pretty as you . . . well . . .'

'You almost make me think I should dye my hair and get some really frumpy clothes,' Kelly had replied, only slightly tongue in cheek. In her own eyes, she was still too young to want serious involvement with any man, although she wasn't blind to her attractiveness. Even the red hair and freckles she often hated couldn't offset a truly pretty face, tidy and sensual figure and a pleasant personality that drew far more men than it repelled.

'Not worth the trouble,' her father had replied. 'You could be flat-chested, bow-legged and have false teeth and only one eye and you'd still be able to find a husband within six months. With your looks I'll be surprised if you're not snapped up before I get out of this damned bed. I surely won't have to worry about Marcel keeping an eye on Kakwa camp, at any rate. One look at you and I'll be lucky to persuade him to leave there!'

And when Marcel Leduc arrived to meet Kelly on the appointed morning, she wasn't that sure she wanted him to leave. He was very tall, perhaps five foot eleven, and slender with that Gallic grace she had encountered during her work in France. Fair hair with a reddish tinge crowned a lean, saturnine face with piercing blue eyes and a sensuous mouth. And despite his being French-Canadian instead of the classic continental Frenchman, it was the Gallic influence she noticed most. He had an instant charm that fairly oozed sexuality, and his eyes undressed her even before he opened his mouth in greeting.

'Your pictures don't do you justice at all,' he remarked in flawless English, then proceeded to devour her with his eyes as she poured them each a cup of coffee. Less appreciated was the somewhat ribald comment he muttered to himself in French, although Kelly supposed it was really more complimentary than otherwise since he had presumed she didn't understand it.

Still, she found his attractiveness somewhat disturbing, and she wasn't overly upset at finally being helped into her father's pick-up truck, in which she was to follow Marcel's vehicle on the long drive southward. It was likely to take them about four hours for the journey, Marcel told her, most of it on the last thirty miles of roughly-formed track through the mountainous terrain near the camp. Even without knowing that terrain, she didn't envy Marcel his own task that day; he'd already driven more than a hundred road miles in from the camp to Grande Prairie, and would be coming all the way back to the city for a second time that day after getting her settled in and the week's supplies delivered.

Kelly paid particular attention to the road, knowing that it would be her task, the following Wednesday, to make the long return trip for essential supplies. Weather permitting, of course; if rain made the road dangerous or impassable, a helicopter would be used for the trip.

Personally, she hoped that wouldn't happen until she had managed to become totally familiar with the route, despite her father's assurances that it was almost impossible to get lost.

The first part of the journey was certainly easy enough. They headed south on a broad, well-made road that dipped through spruce-covered sandhills before crossing the Wapiti River and rising again to the settlements on the other side. Actually, settlements was stretching a point, since for the most part they were only small, rough homesteads carved from the jungle of dark green pine and spruce forest. The settled area didn't last long, either. Soon after they had passed the South Wapiti ranger station all evidence of human activity except the road itself disappeared.

The road, still broad and well gravelled, travelled the ridges where it could, but it dropped down to cross over first Pinto Creek and then Nose Creek before lifting again into what Kelly realised were the first real foothills. Off to her right she could see the beginnings of the proper mountains, and between herself and the rising peaks was the broad expanse of a substantial river valley.

They crested Chinook Ridge, following the ridge for miles with extensive views on both sides of them, views of rugged, timber-covered hills that stretched away into the distance. It was, she thought, like some areas of Scotland and Wales, although different in its total isolation. How easy to imagine that only a few miles from this road there might be trails where no man had ever been before.

When the road slid down the mountain again to the jewelled beauty of two tiny little mountain lakes, Kelly was overjoyed to find that Marcel had halted his truck at a campsite on the shore of the second one.

'The road gets a bit rougher after this,' he said when she had alighted to join him. 'I thought it would be easier on you if we took a break.' He reached into the cab of his truck to emerge with the Thermos bottles of coffee she had prepared before leaving home, and they walked down to sit on a log beside the water.

A pair of red squirrels chattered angrily in the tall pine trees, and no sooner had they got settled than a swift, raucous bird that looked like a grey-coloured blue jay swooped down to perch on a stump and stare at them suspiciously. When Kelly tossed down some pieces of the cookie she was eating, the bird was on them like a shot, crying his pleasure in shrill screams.

'Whisky-jack,' Marcel informed without her asking. 'Actually it's a Canada jay, but you'll never hear them called that out here. Every camp has at least one; we've got a whole flock of them up at Kakwa, and every one of them's an accomplished thief.'

'I think he's delightful,' Kelly replied, 'but why are they called whisky-jacks?'

'No idea,' he shrugged. 'Some of the real old-timers call them camp robbers, and that is accurate enough. They can be a real pest at times.' He snorted angrily. 'If it was left to me I'd shoot a few of them just to get some peace, but Scofield would have my head on a platter if I did.'

'I'm certainly pleased Mr Scofield and I will have one point of agreement from the start,' Kelly said dryly. 'I've been worrying just a bit about my reception. My father hasn't actually come out and said so, but I got the distinct feeling he doesn't expect I'll be welcomed with open arms. Why would that be? I wonder. Just because I'm female?'

Marcel's reply was a bark of laughter not unlike that of the cheeky whisky-jack.

'I don't think that would bother him at all,' he laughed. 'The old grey wolf eats little girls like you for breakfast, or at least that's what some of his men would have you believe. Scofield has a fair reputation as a womaniser, although usually he doesn't attempt to mix business and pleasure. But then I doubt if he's ever had a woman as pretty as you right there in camp with him. From what I understand Scofield doesn't think much of having women in his camps . . . too much of a distraction for the men, if nothing else.'

'But there's already a woman at the camp,' Kelly replied with a troubled glance. 'Mrs . . .'

'Cardinal,' Marcel reminded her. 'And she hardly counts, when you consider she's a wrinkled old métis woman who's fifty if she's a day, looks seventy-five, and has a dozen grown-up kids—not to mention a husband who's there at the camp with her. Marie is your bull-cook and her husband Etienne is sort of general handyman.'

Kelly could tell by the expression on Marcel's face that he expected her to query him about the unfamiliar terminology, and resolved to disappoint him.

She had spent every spare minute during every one of her father's yearly visits to England in questioning him about his work, and she knew very well that a bull-cook, in Canadian terms, was a cook's helper, a sort of kitchen slave who peeled the potatoes, washed the dishes and did most of the heavy labour in camp kitchens.

But she wasn't quite so confident in her ability to deal with the obvious problem of this Scofield man and his attitude that women in a camp led to trouble. Nor did

Kelly really know how to combat such an attitude, except
by the example of simply not causing problems. Certainly,
she thought, she was old enough to handle the attentions of
a group of hard-working prospectors and surveyors, who
should normally be working too hard to have time for
amorous intentions.

Someone like Marcel, she realised instinctively, could be
less easy to deal with, and she was suddenly very glad
indeed that he wasn't going to be on hand at Kakwa camp
every day of the week. Quite an abrupt shift from her
initial impression, she knew, but undoubtedly a safer one,
at least until she came to know him better. The way he kept
looking at her was distinctly unnerving, and she decided it
was high time they started driving again.

As they walked back towards the trucks, Kelly couldn't
help turning back for another look at the placid blue waters
of the small lake. What a pity Kakwa camp couldn't be in a
setting like this, she thought, then spoke without conscious
awareness.

'Is it anything like this—at the camp, I mean?'

'Not at all,' Marcel replied with a wry grin. 'No lake, for
starters, and it's about a thousand feet higher. We're just
on the edge of the real mountains here; at Kakwa you'd be
up over the five-thousand-foot line, I think.'

He grinned at her expression of dismay. 'You wouldn't
want the camp anywhere near here if it was the weekend,'
he said. 'You can't move for the crowds and you can't hear
for the racket. It's the farthest thing imaginable from what
you'd consider unspoiled wilderness. Up on the Kakwa it's
at least quiet some of the time, although even there you've
got the generators and trucks coming and going at all hours
of the day and night.'

Kelly could well believe it. There had hardly been a mile
on the journey south in which they hadn't met or been
passed by some form of vehicle, most of them going exceptionally fast for the rough, dusty road. But it was certainly

in keeping with her father's comments that Grande Prairie was a boom town, and that it would get even worse as exploration and development of the wilderness to the south intensified.

'I hate to see it in a lot of ways,' he had said on the morning after Kelly's disturbing encounter at the school. 'But we need the resources; progress can't be halted that easily. And actually there's no reason why development can't be combined with good conservation practices and resource management. It only needs the right kind of leadership and regulations. That's one of the things I really like about Scofield, his attitude towards conservation.'

Kelly had told her father only enough about the disruptions at the meeting so that he knew there had been a violent protest. Of her own involvement, and her subsequent encounter with the police and the tall grey-eyed stranger, she'd said nothing at all. And when he began to expound about the conservation practices of the Scofield business empire, she thought it just as well to remain silent, since it would only upset Geoff Barnes to hear about the incident. Clearly he thought very highly of this man Scofield, and as he detailed the man's ideas on conservation as he himself knew them, Kelly found herself increasingly impressed.

Her own attitudes towards resource development were firmly entrenched by the ruined countryside left by gravel-stripping and surface mining operations in Britain and by her own studies. She firmly believed in progress, but was becoming increasingly convinced that reclamation costs and planning must be included in any development scheme right from the start. It was heartening to hear her father describe the approach taken by Scofield, who insisted on reclaiming his camps and development sites even though he was under no obligation to do the job as thoroughly as he always did.

'I know of one camp he used for five years straight,' her father had said, 'and if you went back there now you'd never believe there'd ever been a camp on the site. Not like some of these old drilling sites that will be junk heaps for another fifty years.'

Marcel reached into his truck cab to replace the Thermos flasks, and when he emerged he had a rolled-up chart in his hands which he spread out across the hood of the truck.

'Have a look,' he suggested, and Kelly leaned over to watch as his finger traced their route on the forestry map.

'Here's Grande Prairie, and the road we've driven on. And here we are now—Two Lakes. Very original, whoever named them,' he added with a laugh.

Then he showed her the route they must take to reach the camp, his finger following a track pencilled in amongst the dotted lines of seismograph lines and trails. According to the map, the actual road ended at the forestry airstrip at Sherman Meadows, but Marcel's route continued south over Stinking Creek, Mouse Cache Creek, into Dead Horse Meadows and then up the Kakwa River almost to the B.C. border.

'It's a rough old road once we get past Sherman Meadows, so take it easy,' he warned her. 'But don't worry, I'll be keeping an eye out for you if you run into problems.'

He was keeping an eye on her for more reasons than that, Kelly suspected, but she accepted his caution without comment and a few minutes later she was back in the big pick-up truck and following his vehicle down a road that grew increasingly rougher.

Her wrists were aching from the unaccustomed effort of driving such a large vehicle by the time they rounded the final turn in the track to see the buildings of Kakwa camp.

The camp was more or less what Kelly had expected. Three sides of a huge square were taken up with large house-trailers while the gravelled area between them served as a communal parking lot. The left-hand row was the bunk-house accommodation for the men; the centre section housed the kitchen, dining hall, wash-house and laundry facilities, and the right-hand leg held the trailers used for offices and what her father had jokingly called executive accommodation. It was there that the combined office and sleeping quarters that Kelly would use was located.

Obviously the lunch-hour had ended, and there was only a single pick-up truck and a battered old Chevrolet car in the parking lot, but when the two newcomers had parked their vehicles close to the cookhouse, they were immediately greeted by a short, stout and very wrinkled dark woman who Kelly presumed must be Marie Cardinal. To Kelly's surprise the woman literally ignored her, shouting at Marcel in a vivid mixture of French patois and what Kelly thought must be some local Indian language. In any event, she couldn't understand more than a few words of the diatribe, and it became immediately obvious that Marcel couldn't get much out of it either.

Finally, however, he managed to calm the woman down enough so that her rapid speech shifted entirely into French, and it soon became evident what the problem was. The second cook had received a visitor from town soon after Marcel had left that morning, and the visitor had brought whisky—or at least alcohol of some sort.

'So both your cooks are drunk as the proverbial skunk,' he explained eventually, 'and also out of a job, although somehow I doubt if they care much right now. They're both in the cooks' bunkhouse, dead to the world. Frankly, I'm just as glad for the excuse to fire them both, but I can't help wishing they'd picked a better time. I absolutely must go back to Grande Prairie tonight; I have to be in Peace River before noon tomorrow.'

Angrily, Marcel ran his long fingers through the mop of his shaggy hair, sighing with obvious exasperation.

'God, but I hate to leave you with a situation like this,' he sighed. 'In fact, I can't. There's simply no way you can cope with cooking for eighteen men, even with Marie's help. And certainly not when you've only got four hours to get dinner ready for them.'

'I can—and I will,' Kelly replied with a determined gleam in her eye. She had avoided letting Marcel understand that she spoke and understood French almost as well as he, but she wasn't going to allow him to get her started in her work on the wrong foot. 'You just arrange to have your truck unloaded—there's fresh meat and other things that must be put away immediately,' she said. 'And since you're taking my father's truck back, all I ask is that you take your two drinkers back with you. I don't even want to see them, and you can sort out their wages back in town.'

'It's simply too much for you,' he protested. 'I'll get on the blower and arrange something, but I'm going to stay and see things under control.'

He looked around him wildly, and Kelly suddenly realised that he was closer to panic about the situation than she was herself. And obviously the reason was his inability to accept that she could, and would, cope. A meal for eighteen men in four hours wasn't impossible; it simply meant they would have to be less choosy than usual. But what she did want—and must have—was the opportunity to sort out the problem in her own way. She knew only too well that she couldn't afford to have her authority in question so early in the piece. It would be next to impossible for her later on.

'No, you will not stay,' she said imperiously. 'You will get those two drunken sots into the back of that truck and you will get them out of here. If you hurry, you might even get back into town early enough to start looking for a couple of new cooks, which would be very nice indeed as I don't fancy running the camp and cooking three meals a day for ever. Now please, Marcel, will you just get on with it?'

Then she turned to the startled Marie Cardinal and

ordered her to fetch her husband immediately and make a
start at getting the supplies unloaded, as well as showing
her to the company trailer so that she could get changed
and start work.

Both the Metis woman and Marcel stood in awe at the
crackling Parisian French that Kelly used, but the shock
lasted only a moment before Marie Cardinal was scurrying
to obey.

Within half an hour, the worst was over. Marcel had
chivvied the two drunken cooks into Geoff Barnes' pick-up
truck and headed back to town, Marie had bullied her
tiny, silent husband into unloading the supply truck, and
Kelly had thrown her suitcases into the trailer where she
would be living and changed into one of the dozen light
cotton jump-suits she had brought for working in.

It was in the act of changing that the riskiness of her
decision finally struck Kelly, and she shuddered at the
potential for disaster she had created. But it was too late for
recrimination, she could only go forward and pray for the
best. Squaring her shoulders beneath the jump-suit, she
trotted across to the cook-shack and cajoled the other
woman into showing her where things were and how the
equipment worked.

It took a fair bit of negotiation—Marie's French was
substantially different from what Kelly had learned and
even her English was often open to misinterpretation, while
Kelly, of course, understood none of the stout woman's
rapid Cree. But they took an immediate liking to each
other once Marcel was off the site, and when the first of the
men arrived just before six o'clock, they had managed to
put together a quite acceptable meal.

That it wasn't exactly what the men were used to, Kelly
guessed by the expressions on the first faces at the servery.
And she took their expressions of delight as being caused by
the food, rather than her own somewhat dishevelled appearance.

A look at the larder and the chef's menus had told her already the awful news that the men of the Scofield operation had been surviving on steak and potatoes and steak and potatoes and steak and potatoes. Certainly a boring diet, she thought, and quite an illogical one considering the quantities of frozen chickens and fish and various vegetables she found in one of the two huge camp freezers. And she was thankful for the fresh produce and meats that had come with herself and Marcel that morning.

It meant she had been able to provide a choice of two salads, fresh fried chicken and/or tiny lamb chops, mashed potatoes and a mixture of turnip and carrot for vegetables. Dessert hadn't been quite so easy, but she had found enough frozen cream cakes in the freezer to get through a few days, until she either got new cooks or time to get some baking done.

Her biggest problem had been judging quantity, and she had chosen to simply double what she thought reasonable by generous restaurant standards and add ten per cent for good measure. It might mean some waste, but better that than to have too little.

The entire operation was a rush to deadline, so she hardly noticed when the first arrivals only glanced through the servery and turned to leave the dining room. Obviously, she thought, they had only come to check if there was time to wash up properly before eating, although she was vaguely surprised nobody spoke to her.

It wasn't until Kelly had finished loading the steam trays and making her final checks that all was ready that Marie drew her attention to the gathering crowd outside. The woman's patois made it difficult for Kelly to get her message at first, but her own observation through the window made it clear enough.

These men hadn't merely gone to clean up for dinner; most of them looked as if they were geared up for a night on the town. And when the first of them entered the dining room, shyly at first but with growing bravado and sheer noise as the numbers provided security, Kelly suddenly realised that she herself was at least as much of an attraction as the food.

Her first reaction was to flee back to her trailer and get cleaned up herself. With a smudge of something on her forehead and her fresh jump-suit quite messed up after an afternoon of slaving in the kitchen, she didn't feel at all up to meeting the stares and curiosity of this rather startling group of men. Her second reaction was to laugh at their often juvenile escapades; they looked for all the world like a flock of bantam roosters on parade for a single hen. Herself, which was a frighteningly sober thought.

But her third reaction was the best, at least from her own viewpoint. Clearly she must establish some form of control, and as the cacophony of hoots and laughter subsided for a moment she stuck her head through the servery and spoke in her most polished B.B.C. accent.

'Dinnnnah . . . is served!'

The result wasn't quite what she had expected. Instead of the orderly line-up she had expected at the servery, there was only a moment's stunned silence and then the rumble of feet as the stampede approached. In the pandemonium before her she could see only disaster, and without conscious thought she reached up, slammed down the hatch of the servery, then strode through the adjacent doorway into the dining room to stand, hands on hips, facing the startled throng.

'What do you think this is, a hog trough?' she demanded of the man closest to her.

A blond giant of about nineteen, he simply stood and stared at her, his soft blue eyes so full of a longing for something besides food that Kelly was shaken at the intensity. Faltering, she turned to the next closest man, and with a deep breath before she spoke, demanding to know what the reason was for such outrageous behaviour.

He, too, was silent, but somewhere from the back of the throng somebody muttered quite clearly, 'Man, oh, man, wait until the old grey wolf faces up to this little red fox!' It drew a half-hearted bout of laughter from the back of the room, but those directly facing Kelly only looked bewildered . . . and incredibly shy.

'Well, if he doesn't behave any better than you lot, he'll be going to bed hungry,' she snapped. 'Now line up and let's get at it before everything's cold.'

It was all she could do to keep a straight face when she flung open the servery again to meet the soulful blue eyes of her young Nordic giant, who headed up an arrow-straight line of silent, embarrassed men. Each in his turn took up his cutlery and tray and stood before Kelly as she dished up for them, but not one of them spoke a single word except please, no, or thank you in response to her questions. And not a single one took his eyes from her for an instant.

Silently they came, and silently they retreated to the tables, where there was considerable jockeying for seats that allowed a clear view of the servery. It wasn't until halfway through the meal that at least some of the men resumed a semblance of normality and began to discuss their day's work and other topics.

Marie was clearly impressed by the whole performance, and managed to convey to Kelly her approval of the way she had whipped the crew into shape. Clearly, Kelly was going to be a very popular addition to the camp, she said in her patois, very sexy, very pretty, but very tough. You might well approve, Kelly thought to herself, but it's me who's shaking in my boots!

'Is that all, then?' she asked after the last one had taken his loaded tray and departed.

'Oh no. Still the boss yet. He comes soon,' Marie replied, and Kelly shrugged and began putting lids on the steam trays.

'Well, I hope he isn't too long, or this isn't going to be

the best meal he's ever eaten,' she sighed.

Kelly was exhausted. Her feet hurt, her legs were trembling from the combination of the long day's drive and having been on her feet ever since, and she knew she looked and felt a proper mess. Breaking her own rule about smoking in the kitchen—just this once, she promised—she slumped on to a handy stool and relaxed, trying to summon enough strength to carry on with her work.

The voices in the dining room seemed to float out of nothingness, but enough of the kaleidoscope of voices filtered through to inform her that most of the men had enjoyed the change in menu, and that they were enjoying the new cook even more.

Just as well I didn't get tidied up, she mused with a grin, or half of them wouldn't be able to eat at all! There was something incredibly satisfying about such wholesale adulation, but it had a frightening side as well, and she could easily appreciate her father's warning about being in a camp of woman-hungry men. She was having a marvellous fantasy about picking out the strongest to defend her from the rest when a sudden silence from outside brought her back to reality with a jolt.

It didn't need much imagination to realise the cause. The boss had arrived. A gravelly voice confirmed it a second later.

'What the hell is going on here?' it demanded. 'God, the place smells like a Chinese cat-house!'

The sarcastic comment made Kelly suddenly aware of the sweetish odour she had been noticing since dinner began, but had been too busy to clarify. After-shave! And worse, cheap after-shave in cloying over-abundance.

Her nose wrinkled both in distaste and laughter as she sprang to her feet and started loading a plate from the steam trays. A glance at the quantities made her suddenly hopeful that at least some of the men would be back for seconds; there seemed to be an awful lot left. Maybe after the boss had his share, she thought idly, then looked up to take his order.

'Chicken or lamb chops or . . .'

'Both, please,' said that suddenly all-too-familiar voice, and Kelly dropped the plate as her eyes saw that craggy face, that frosty grey hair and those piercing, icy grey eyes.

The plate bounced off the edge of the mashed potatoes compartment before slithering in two pieces into the fried chicken, but Kelly never even noticed. It seemed that her entire being was locked by her eyes to the man before her, a man who said nothing more, merely raised one sooty eyebrow and glanced significantly towards the rack of clean plates.

It took all of Kelly's will to help her wrench free her eyes and reach with shaking fingers to fumble up another plate which she filled to his directions.

Scofield! Grey Scofield? Him! Her mind whirled at the implications, and her legs went all strange at the thought. She barely managed to survive the next twenty minutes as man after man returned for second helpings until the trays were empty except for a single tiny chicken wing.

Kelly had been too busy to even think of eating, and her unexpected encounter with Grey Scofield would have driven hunger from her in any event, but somehow the sight of that lonely piece of chicken made her stomach scream with emptiness and she started to salivate like a Pavlovian dog.

Unthinking, she reached out to take it in the tongs, and was just about to pick it up when a movement caught her side-vision and she looked up to see Grey Scofield standing there, plate outstretched. Her stomach flipped over, then howled in protest as she gave the pale-eyed boss a sickly smile and dropped the chicken wing onto his plate. And when he didn't move, she reached out and took the plate from his fingers, moving quickly across the line of trays to heap on to it the remaining potatoes and vegetables.

Grey Scofield took it with a mocking, insolent nod and returned to his seat, and Kelly swung away from the servery with a shudder of repressed anger. She looked at the growing stack of dirty dishes, thought vaguely about dirtying still more to fix up something for herself, then threw her hands up in total despair. It was just too much trouble. Marie had taken plates for herself and her husband, so that wasn't a problem. Kelly gave up.

She waited only long enough to instruct Marie on the cleaning up, then fled out the back of the dining trailer to her own unit, where she slammed the door and threw herself on to the bed as the tears began to flow.

She didn't cry for long; tearful hysterics had never been much in Kelly's line and she was angrily ashamed at her own weakness within minutes. Rising, red-eyed and flushed, she flung open her suitcases and stripped off the soiled jump-suit before grabbing up her wrap and moving into the small trailer bathroom. With a mental thanks to her father, she turned on the shower and stood under it for what seemed like an hour, allowing the steaming water to sooth away her tiredness and the strain in her muscles.

To hell with Grey Scofield; to hell with everything, she thought as she wrapped the towel around her and stepped out into the main area of the trailer. Tomorrow would be soon enough—too soon—to work things out. She was just reaching for her wrap when the entire trailer shuddered to the tread of heavy feet on the steps and the door was flung open to admit the head and shoulders of the one man she wanted least to see at this particular moment.

'Leduc! Just what the hell is that redheaded high school horror doing here in my camp?' Grey Scofield demanded before he'd so much as looked to see who was in the trailer.

And when he did look, there wasn't a hint of apology in the steely eyes that frankly appraised Kelly's scantily-covered figure and startled, wide-eyed face. The two of them stared at each other in silence for a moment, and it was Kelly who spoke first.

'You might have knocked,' she said through clenched teeth.

Grey Scofield merely lifted that hateful eyebrow in a gesture of obvious disdain for her growing anger.

'I'm just as glad I didn't,' he said, the soft words dripping with innuendo as he contained his appraisal. Kelly felt as if she were naked on an auction block, despite her certain knowledge that the towel covered her at least as adequately as any dressing gown would have.

She stood, trembling with both anger and something far more primitive, the recognition of this grey-haired young man's startling masculinity and her own reaction to it. Grey said nothing, but Kelly could see his chest heaving beneath the tidy khaki shirt and the pulse throbbing in his throat as he undressed her with his eyes.

'Will you get *out* of here!' she cried in sudden panic, half turning to flee, but flee where? Grey Scofield was standing in the only door the trailer had, and behind her was only a huge double bed that suddenly seemed to loom like a trap.

'Where's Leduc?' His voice was strangely gentle, but Kelly started violently as he moved further into the trailer, slipping into a casual slouch against the counter in the office section.

'He's in Grande Prairie, I expect,' she replied with equal and unexpected calm.

'And what is he doing in Grande Prairie when he's supposed to be here in charge of this camp?'

'I'm in charge here now,' she replied with a slight lift of her head as she tensed for the explosion that had to come. And it did.

CHAPTER TWO

GREY SCOFIELD jerked erect with a loud and violent oath, and before Kelly could move had crossed the space between them in a single, pantherish leap to grasp her by the upper arms and lift her so that their eyes were on the same level. With both hands frantically trying to keep the towel around her, she struggled for only an instant before his piercing eyes commanded her to immobility.

'All right, sweetie, now let's just cut the nonsense,' he growled in a menacing voice. 'If you want to come out here and shack up with that French cradle-robber, that's your business, but don't try and hand me a bunch of garbage about being in charge of *my* camp. Now what in the hell's going on?'

Kelly went cold inside at the unfairness of his charge, and the anger completely overshadowed her uniquely vulnerable position. Even more surprising, it suddenly cleared away the fear she had felt when Grey had picked her up.

'Put me down,' she said in a voice quite as fierce as his own, and quite as deathly soft. When he didn't move after several seconds, but merely stared into her eyes, she made a quick mental judgment about where she would kick him, and even shifted her right foot back a few inches.

'I wouldn't, if I were you,' he said in what was almost a whisper.

'Then put me down,' she replied with deadly calm. 'Now!'

'And if I don't?'

'Then I shall kick you where it hurts the most,' Kelly replied in total seriousness.

30

'After warning me first?' Grey Scofield shook his head, a wry grin softening his features. 'You must be even younger than you look.'

And to her surprise, he deposited her so gently, so lightly to the floor that she didn't feel her feet touch it. Then he backed away to his original lounging stance against the counter, where he stood glaring at her with obvious disgust.

'What are you—Leduc's daughter or something?' he asked harshly.

'I am not his daughter; and I am most certainly not, as you so crudely put it, shacked up with him either,' Kelly retorted haughtily. 'I am . . .'

'Well, you must be somebody's daughter,' Grey interrupted. 'And whoever he is, he's got my sympathy. Dammit, child, just what do you think your father would think if he were here right now? If it was me, I'd paddle your pretty little backside until you couldn't sit down for a month!'

Kelly took a deep breath, struggling to hold her temper long enough to get some sanity into this outrageous conversation.

'My father——' she began very slowly and calmly, and then as he appeared about to interrupt, 'Will you please just shut up and listen to me!' Her shriek had the desired effect, and his mouth closed long enough for her to continue.

'My father,' she said again, 'would probably be wondering—as I am—whatever insanity prompted him to say that you were one of the finest men he knows. Because he obviously doesn't know you very well, or he'd have warned me that you're insufferable, arrogant, ignorant and . . . and stupid!'

She could feel the tears coming, and struggled for control as he raised one eyebrow and looked at her without saying a word. Kelly blinked back the tears as the silence continued, and finally burst out, 'Well, aren't you going to say anything?'

'Your opinion of me is as irrelevant as it's obvious,' he replied calmly. 'What I want to know is who the hell are you and what are you doing here? And until I know that I couldn't care less what either you or your father thinks.'

Kelly gritted her teeth, biting back yet another angry retort. Obviously, she thought, her verbal assault on this strange man had been underplayed, or else he was simply too thick-skinned to bother with it.

'I am Kelly Barnes,' she finally replied in a slow, specific fashion. 'My father is Geoff Barnes. He is the owner of this catering firm. He is in the hospital in Grande Prairie. While he is in the hospital, I am in charge of this camp. This is his trailer; therefore it is now *my* trailer. Now will you kindly *get out of here!*'

From Grey Scofield's silence, she had presumed that finally she had managed to get through to him, and that finally he would accept her authority—and her order to leave the trailer. He did neither.

Instead, he stayed silently regarding her for what seemed like hours before he finally spoke.

'You did that very well,' he said solemnly. 'Almost well enough to be convincing.'

The evident sarcasm spurred Kelly's response.

'What do you mean?' she cried.

'I mean that you're a pretty fair actress; Leduc has coached you really well,' he said. 'But you both forgot one thing—Geoff's daughter is a grown woman and a fully qualified caterer, not a high-school rabble-rouser.'

Kelly was stunned by the accusation. The conservation meeting incident notwithstanding, she simply couldn't accept that this man could be so stubbornly blind as to flatly reject her explanation. But obviously he wasn't accepting it; his dictatorial silence clearly demanded some other explanation.

She took a deep breath and drew herself up to the limit of her diminutive height, a gesture that lost most of its dignity when she had to clutch at the slipping, half-forgotten towel. It took every ounce of her self-control to restrain herself from screaming when he grinned patronisingly at the gesture, but when she spoke, it was with total calmness.

'I'm twenty-four. I'm a fully qualified caterer and I'm a Cordon Bleu chef,' she replied. 'And no matter what you may think, *Mister* Scofield, I am Geoff Barnes' daughter. Would you like to see my passport, my certificates, my driver's licence? Or since you've eaten my cooking, perhaps you'd just like to take my word for it—because it's the *last* meal you'll get in this camp until I get an apology.'

The calmness evaporated as her last few words rose with her temper, and she was subconsciously looking for something to throw at him when Grey Scofield surprised her by grinning at her with an expression of genuine delight.

'Well, I'll be damned!' he said, straightening to his full height before folding his arms across his broad chest and leaning back to regard her with new interest. 'It was *you* that cooked that truly splendid meal tonight?'

Kelly's expression was answer enough, which was just as well, because his look of honest admiration had thrown her for such a loop she couldn't speak. Smiling, he looked not only a good deal younger than when he was angry, but very much more handsome. There was a small-boy attractiveness there which clutched at Kelly's heart, and a mature masculinity that strengthened that grip despite her anger. She was still searching for words when he unfolded his arms and spoke again.

'You'll be more likely to think of forgiving me if I give you a chance to get dressed,' he said with a grin. 'Meanwhile I'll rustle us up a drink, provided that Frenchman didn't drink up all of your dad's whisky.'

Before Kelly realised what was happening, he picked up her suitcases and carefully set them on the bed beside her, made a second trip for her handbag, then reached up to close the sliding curtain-door that separated the bedroom section from the rest of the trailer, giving her an exaggerated bow as he did so.

When she slid open the curtain a few minutes later, feeling far more comfortable in one of her slack suits and a light cotton blouse, she found him slouched comfortably in one of the trailer's easy chairs, a glass of something in one hand and a cigarette in the other. He rose politely to his feet as she stepped into the room.

'Hope you like Scotch; it's all there was,' he said, reaching out for her hand as he escorted her gallantly into the other chair and then handed her a glass that looked to hold more Scotch than water. Kelly sipped at it cautiously; his act was wearing just a trifle thin and she was finding that suspicion had replaced her anger. She had never met anybody so changeable and yet so totally in-control of himself, nor anybody who had such a strong masculine attraction for her, she admitted silently. The transition from tyrant to slave to gentleman was somewhat unnerving.

And what was worse, she strongly suspected this grey-eyed, grey-haired, grey-named mystery man was doing his level best to set her up for something. But what? Surely he realised she wouldn't dare abide by her angry threat to bar him from her dining room. He wasn't stupid, regardless of what she had said about him. As the pleasant warmth of the whisky streamed down inside her, she quirked her mouth wryly and leaned back in the chair. Let him make the first move.

'First of all, I do seriously apologise,' he said after a moment's silence in which each of them assessed the other from a viewpoint far different than their earlier ones.

'And I accept,' Kelly replied softly.

'Does that mean I get breakfast?' His grin was contagious.

'I guess so,' she said with a smile of her own.

'Thank you.'

'You're welcome,' she replied, thinking, this is really silly. It's ridiculous, in fact. We can't sit here trading inanities like this.

'When is Marcel Leduc coming back?' He had to repeat himself twice before Kelly shook herself from her own thoughts to answer him.

'I . . . I'm not sure. When I need him, I hope. But we made no specific plans. He has the various other camps to supervise, as I imagine you know.'

'Hmph. How's your father?'

'He's recovering, but it could be a month before he leaves hospital,' she replied. What is he leading up to, anyway? she thought.

'And you're going to administer things here. Alone? And do the cooking as well?'

The pattern started to become clearer, and Kelly steeled herself for the objections she expected.

'For the moment,' she replied. 'Marcel is supposed to be looking for two new cooks. I fired the two drunkards who were here when we arrived today.'

She half expected that remark to draw a strong response, but he only grunted admiringly. 'Saved me the trouble,' he said then. 'I'd have done it if you hadn't.'

It was calculated to get a rise, and Kelly knew it, but she couldn't help retorting, 'By what authority, may I ask?'

'My authority, Miss Barnes,' he replied softly, and the lines of his face told her it was an authority only a fool would question.

'But they were our employees, not yours,' she retorted, almost flinching in expectation of a blast. Surprisingly, it didn't come.

'It's *my* camp,' he said quietly. 'And it's a dry camp—no booze allowed, and no exceptions. What the men do in town is their own affair, but they don't bring liquor into camp or they're out on their ears.'

Kelly looked at Grey Scofield, then reached down to pick up her glass, sip at her whisky, and replace the glass with a significant thud on the table.

'And do we go separately, or together?' she asked with a derisive grin. The grin widened at his look of astonishment.

'*Touché!*' he nodded after a moment's silence. 'But I think we can consider this a medical emergency. It's certainly been a drink-deserving shock to me. And besides, being the boss does entail *some* privileges.'

'I hope that applies to the cook as well,' she replied wryly. 'I wouldn't fancy trying to make coq au vin with fruit juices instead of wine.'

'After today's performance . . .' he paused to grin engagingly at her immediate stiffening, '. . . I would be run out of camp on a rail if I dared to question *anything* you did in your kitchen, Miss Barnes. Which puts me in something of a difficult position . . .'

He let the comment drag out as if expecting a response, but Kelly leaned back in her chair and waited silently for him to continue. It wouldn't be all his way, she vowed, knowing there was something coming she wouldn't like.

'I can see you're not going to make it easy for me,' he said finally. 'Okay, we'll do it your way. I'd like you to go back to Grande Prairie.'

'Right this minute?' Kelly replied with a deliberate obtuseness.

'As soon as is reasonably possible.' It was a blunt, yet somehow gentle statement, obviously calculated to make her ask why.

'*Now* is reasonably possible,' she replied. 'But are you capable of getting breakfast for eighteen men? And lunch, and dinner tomorrow? Or hadn't you thought of that, *Mister* Scofield?'

'Now don't get snarly, little fox,' he said with a grin. 'There's been enough misunderstandings already today . . .'

'And all of them yours,' she snapped back.

Grey Scofield lifted his eyebrow and scowled at her in what might have been mock anger. He was about to speak when she interrupted.

'And just for the record, Mr Scofield, I am not a fox,' she said sternly.

He laughed, causing her to once again recognise just how truly handsome he could be. 'You're one of the foxiest ladies I've ever run across,' he chuckled. 'And according to my boys in the dining hall tonight, you are the . . . original . . . red fox. You should take that as a compliment, by the way.'

'That was their stomachs talking,' she replied, grimacing at the remembrance of what she had looked like in the kitchen, with stained overall, smudged face and no make-up.

'Today, true enough,' Grey admitted. 'But it's tomorrow and the next day that worries me. And next week even more, because once the novelty wears off you're going to mean nothing but trouble for me, Miss Barnes.'

'You mean I'm going to become a sex object,' she replied tartly. 'And you don't think I can handle that?'

'Frankly, no, I don't,' he said.

'Your confidence is overwhelming,' she sneered.

'And so is your naïveté.'

Kelly flared visibly. 'I've been dealing with men through-out my working life,' she said angrily. 'And may I remind you, Mr Scofield, that I may look rather young, but I'm no longer a child. I can take care of myself quite comfortably, thank you.'

Grey was unperturbed. 'Well, maybe where you come from it works your way,' he replied with a grin, 'but out here you've got to kick *before* you caution. Any one of that bunch of roughnecks out there would eat you for break-fast.'

'Funny, that's what I heard them saying about you,'

Kelly replied hotly, then immediately regretted it as he looked at her with sudden speculation.

'And you don't think I would?' he asked with alarming gentleness. 'Don't let anything fool you, Miss Barnes. The way to a man's heart may be through his stomach, but once you get there he's likely to forget about food in preference to other things.'

Kelly had to fight to keep from shrinking back into her chair; the expression in his eyes was all too vividly descriptive. He was undressing her with his eyes, and their touch was almost a physical caress.

'I would have thought you could control yourself quite adequately,' she replied carefully. 'Certainly you couldn't expect to control your men otherwise.'

He grinned at her, but the unholy gleam never left his eyes. 'That wasn't the point,' he said. 'Do you think that *you* could control me?'

'I should hope I wouldn't be placed in a position where it would be necessary,' Kelly replied coldly.

'You're evading the issue.'

'Not at all,' she retorted. 'I simply feel that the control of *your* men is *your* responsibility and I expect you to exercise that responsibility.'

Grey shook his head and grinned at her. 'Very nicely put, but it doesn't answer the question. Nor does it resolve the problem, or hadn't you noticed?'

'I haven't seen any problem,' Kelly replied resolutely. 'And I don't expect to see one, unless you make it. As a matter of fact I think the impression you're trying to create is quite libellous and probably equally unfair. You forget, Mr Scofield, that I've already met your men, and I didn't see a single indication of all this trauma you keep dreaming up.'

'In other words, you think I'm something of a panic merchant.'

Kelly smiled at the thought. 'You might say that,' she murmured.

'And you're quite sure you can handle this . . . mythical problem I've dreamed up?'

She didn't like the smile that accompanied the question, but she was in far too deep to back away. 'That's right,' she said.

Grey rose easily to his feet and moved towards the doorway, and Kelly automatically rose and walked over to see him out.

She was barely on her feet, however, when he suddenly spun around to clasp her in arms that crushed the very breath from her as they hugged her against his broad chest. She could feel the heat of his body through her thin blouse and was far too vividly aware of the strong masculine scent of him, a scent of pine and spruce and tobacco . . . and man.

She tried to struggle, but he had moved so that she was backed against the counter; she couldn't get leg room to kick and his arms held her own immobile as he stared down into her eyes with an intense, mocking ferocity. She met his eyes, unable to turn away even though she wanted to, and when his lips descended upon hers, she was helpless to stop them.

At first they were harsh, demanding a response from her without caring what that response might be, but after a moment his mouth softened, exploring her lips and her cheek and her face before returning to caress her mouth with expert skill. His arms pulled her against him, and the touch of his fingers in the small of her back was an exquisite torture that helped to part her lips beneath his as she began to return his kiss.

His fingers became lighter, moving so gently across her back, her shoulders, into her hair and then down to caress her flanks as she fitted herself against him. Her mind was crying stop, but her body no longer listened, and her hands were wound about his neck, her fingers tangled in the thick hair as she pulled herself up to merge her body with his, oblivious to all warnings and heedless of all but their combined desires.

She was only dimly aware that he had lifted her clear of the floor and was moving, until suddenly he bent to deposit her on the huge double bed, his body floating down with her as his kisses held her captive and his hands began a more subtle, intimate exploration.

Sanity returned with a burst of uncontrollable terror as she tried to fling herself away from him, only to find herself pinned by his body and those delightful, frightening, almost irresistible hands. Shaking her body in total panic, she struggled and fought and twisted, first in silence and then with a terrified attempt to scream. But as her mouth opened, he closed it with his own, and her captivity became all the more difficult to fight as she felt his lips soften almost immediately into a caress. His chest flattened her breasts and she could feel his passion rising against her as he used his strength to manoeuvre her flailing body to meet his desires.

Again she tried to scream, and again he stopped her with his kisses, and as her own strength began to fade, Kelly's mind seemed to retreat as well, seeking solace within herself as she gave up the fight and lay passive beneath him. He could take her now, and she realised it, and with that realisation came a renewed instinct to fight, to resist him somehow, anyhow.

But even as her body stiffened in response to that inner crisis demand, he was gone. He had released her and backed away from the bed in a single panther-like gesture, and Kelly looked up to see his large form looming over her.

'Now we both know the answer to my question,' he said very softly, and Kelly was astounded at how aware she was, not only of his voice, but of his heaving chest and the tense, rigid stance that proclaimed his control. And she was also aware, perhaps even more so, of how much her own responses had contributed to the intensity of his lovemaking. Her mind was as bruised as her lips, and the bruising was because she couldn't be totally certain she had really wanted him to stop.

'Aren't you going to say anything?' Grey demanded after what seemed like hours of silence in which their eyes were locked as if by an invisible chain.

'I think you're . . . an animal,' she whispered. 'Get out of here . . . get out . . . get out . . . get out! I could kill you for that! You're totally despicable . . .'

'And now you hate me. Quite a change from five minutes ago, isn't it?' he replied with the ghost of a grin.

'Get out!' Kelly spat. 'You've made your point, now get out.'

'Only part of the point,' he replied with infuriating calm. And then, to her surprise, he walked over and reached down for her hand.

She recoiled as if she had been shot, jerking her hand away before he could touch her. 'Don't you dare touch me!' she snarled. 'If you ever touch me again I'll kill you, I promise you that!'

'And you accuse me of over-dramatising things,' he grinned. 'It's only your pride that I hurt and you know it, so stop being so ridiculously defensive and listen to me.'

It was true, but there was no way on earth that Kelly was going to admit to Grey Scofield just how right he was. 'I can't imagine myself being the slightest bit interested in anything you might want to say,' she replied bitterly.

'You want to stay here in this camp—you'll listen,' he growled, then waved his huge hand in a vague gesture towards the door. 'I want that locked whenever you're in here, day or night. And at night, you'll either be here or with Marie in the cook-shack, unless you're with me. The bunkhouses are off limits, so's the shower block. And after dark, by which time you ought to be in bed like a good little girl anyway, you don't go anywhere alone. Not anywhere—is that clear?'

'Are you sure you wouldn't rather get some chain and a

padlock, so you can either chain me to the stove or lock me up inside here?' Kelly replied hotly.

'If it comes to that, I'll consider it,' was the grim reply. 'While you're here, you're my responsibility whether you like it or not . . .'

'Well, I don't think much of the way you've been upholding your responsibilities,' she interrupted. 'Who's going to protect me from you, while you're so busy protecting me from everybody else?' Gone was her earlier fear of his masculine power; the sheer anger she felt at his autocratic attitude overshadowed everything else.

'*I'll* protect you from me,' Grey said with soft but vivid emphasis. 'What worries me is who's going to protect *me* from *you*. I don't fancy arsenic in my coffee.'

'I'd favour strychnine myself,' she snapped. 'Arsenic is for people, not mangy old wolves.'

To her surprise, Grey laughed delightedly at the retort, and his laugh softened into the boyish smile she had liked so much earlier. 'You're tougher than I thought,' he said with what actually appeared to be honest admiration. 'Now if you were just a little bigger, I wouldn't worry half so much about you.'

'If I were very much bigger, you'd have to worry about yourself,' she replied angrily. 'Now will you please get out of here. I've had a long, difficult day even without your assaults, and I'd like to get some sleep.'

'Do you promise to lock the door behind me?' he asked suspiciously.

'I would like nothing better,' Kelly assured him with a grim shake of her head. 'Unless it was to shoot you.'

'Oh, don't be so snarly about a harmless little object lesson,' he replied. 'It's only your pride that's hurt, and you're young enough to get over that. Hell, by tomorrow you might even like me again.'

'Don't hold your breath,' she murmured as he stepped through the door. Then she rushed to slam it behind him, throwing the bolt in a frenzied movement before she leaned against the counter, panting with a mixture of anger, fear and emotion.

And now that he was safely outside, she began plotting her revenge.

CHAPTER THREE

She soon found out, however, that plotting revenge is far easier said than done, especially for someone like herself who wasn't a vengeful person by nature. In the few minutes before exhaustion claimed her, she thought up and immediately rejected several possibilities, most of them so ridiculous that when she woke in the morning she couldn't but laugh at them.

A 'hot chocolate' drink made from a powerful laxative had seemed appropriate and fitting the night before; in the cold light of dawn it was unseemly cruel. If she had been in charge of the laundry, she would have given somewhat more serious consideration to heavily starching Grey's underwear, but the logistics of that possibility were beyond her.

Obviously, her revenge would have to be a highly personal one, yet not so serious that it would threaten her father's business arrangements with the arrogant Mr Scofield. And it also couldn't be anything that would unduly upset anybody else in the camp. She thought idly of lacing his apple pie with cayenne pepper, but rejected that idea too. Somehow, Kelly knew, she would have to find her revenge in some fashion that made it a private thing between herself and Grey Scofield, some fashion that wouldn't hold him up to public ridicule or scorn—because she knew *that* would be unthinkably dangerous.

Subtlety—that must be the key, she thought as she flew through her shower and headed for the cook-shack to start breakfast preparations.

She became too busy, then, to worry about anything but slicing bacon and whipping up mountains of scrambled

44

eggs and skyscrapers of hot buttered toast. Even when Grey sauntered into the dining room with a careless wave of greeting, she could only return the wave and favour him with a blistering scowl when he finally approached to claim his portion of the breakfast feast.

And she was mightily grateful when he announced that he would have the men return to the camp for lunch that day, since it would have been unreasonable to have expected her to know the camp routine on such short notice and have cut lunches already prepared.

'But why didn't somebody tell me?' she objected, feeling intensely ashamed for not having thought to ask the night before. It was a slur on her own professional standard not to have known, and her embarrassment wasn't aided by the fact that she should have known without being told.

'You didn't really need that kind of burden on top of the day you'd already had—did you?' Grey remarked. And at her vague admission, he laughed in a casual, friendly fashion. 'Look, we're not monsters out here,' he said. 'And we don't ask for miracles, either, although about half the men think the meal they got last night was in the miracle class. Now I want you to pace yourself today. Let Marie take care of lunch; it only has to be sandwiches and coffee, and you see if you match last night's dinner without working yourself to death.'

'I'll be able to do much better than just match it, having the whole day to work in,' she promised. 'And really, I am sorry about not thinking of the lunches. It's purely my own fault; I should have thought of it.'

'About organising it, maybe,' he said. 'But you can't do everything yourself, so until you get your new cooks, let Marie worry about lunches; she has enough time for it. You shouldn't even attempt to consider being administrator and chef as well. You'll only work yourself into the ground to no good purpose.'

Then, to Kelly's immense surprise, he threw her one of his engaging, boyish grins before continuing.

'And if anything has to suffer, let it be the administration. After last night's performance I've got the happiest camp in the country, and I'd like to keep it that way. In fact I'm almost tempted to try and convince Leduc that I'd rather have you here as a cook, and he can find somebody else to handle the administration.'

'I thought you didn't want me here at all,' she replied sarcastically. 'Or is this just your stomach talking?'

Grey shrugged and gestured towards the dining room. 'It's everybody else's stomach that's talking,' he admitted wryly. 'If I tried to get rid of you now, they'd string me up from the closest high tree.'

'Well, judging from your comments last night, maybe you'd prefer that anyway,' she retorted. 'Or are you finally now convinced that I'm not likely to be the troublemaker you envisaged?'

'That depends on how much you learned from last night's little lesson,' he replied smugly, grinning with delight at her angry reaction. 'On the other hand, if I have to keep giving you lessons like that, I might get to enjoy having you around just for the entertainment value.'

Kelly shivered with repressed anger, only just able to restrain herself from throwing something at him. Entertainment value indeed! But she was still struggling to find a suitable reply when Grey suddenly excused himself and walked quickly out of the dining hall. It wasn't until she had finally found time for a filling breakfast of her own that Kelly really began to assess her reaction to his comment, and she was immediately angry with herself for feeling so slighted. What interest could she possibly have in providing 'entertainment' for a man like Grey Scofield? The very thought was enough to make her . . . Oh, you're lucky I didn't poison your coffee, she thought with a derisive gesture at his trailer.

She had cooled down only slightly by the time the men

began to filter into the trailer seeking their lunches, and Grey's arrival made Kelly think of fleeing to hide in her trailer, because she was afraid she would say something quite atrocious if he spoke to her. But when he did finally approach, he wasn't alone. With him was a diminutive, stocky little man hardly taller than Kelly herself, an ageing, wrinkled little fellow who doffed a greasy, ancient cap to reveal a shining bald pate as he smiled a mostly-toothless greeting.

Grey introduced his companion as Baldy Swan. 'Baldy's going to fill in as second cook until you get your new crew,' he explained bluntly. 'He's not a bad cook, actually, although it's a few years since he gave up cooking for cat-skinning. Just don't let him try anything too fancy.'

'Oh, but I . . .'

'And don't go all shirty about it,' he said with a slight scowl. 'Nobody's trying to impugn your abilities or anything. But I don't want you killing yourself with work, and old Baldy here should be able to take some of the load.'

The gleeful look on the older man's face made it clear that he was either pleased at the chance of returning to the kitchen, or else he was simply enjoying the visible air of hostility between Kelly and Grey. He was the nearest thing to a living leprechaun that Kelly had ever seen, and she immediately knew she must avoid hurting his feelings.

'I'm certainly not complaining about the help,' she said immediately. 'I'm certain that Mr Swan can probably teach me a good deal, as a matter of fact.' Her comment brought a glint of appreciation, or was it smugness, into Grey's eyes, and she continued, 'But I don't feel it's proper to take somebody from your staff; I'm sure you need all of your men at your own work . . .'

She paused at the look of speculation that replaced Grey's earlier expression, and he took it to mean she had finished.

'I appreciate your feelings,' he replied. 'But it's not quite that simple. I've got to be away for the next couple of days, and since somebody has to stay and look after you, it might as well be somebody who can be useful to you.'

Kelly was livid. 'So he's really to be my bodyguard!'

'That's right,' Grey replied grimly. 'Which means that his word is *mine*, and you'll treat it as such. Outside the kitchen, of course. And don't let his size fool you, Miss Barnes. Baldy's handled tougher men in his day than any that this camp could produce.'

'I wasn't questioning his abilities,' she replied hotly. 'But I must object to you taking him from his regular duties just because *you* think I need a bodyguard. As I've told you repeatedly, Mr Scofield, I'm quite capable of looking after myself.'

'Well then, Baldy will be able to enjoy taking things easy when he isn't cooking,' was the reply. 'Don't be so snappy, little fox. You're getting to the point where you've no sense of humour at all, and if there's one thing I can't stand it's a grouchy cook; Baldy's cooked for me enough over the years to confirm that.'

'I am not snappy and I'm not a fox,' she retorted. 'And I don't need a bodyguard, so before you go, you can please send Mr Swan back to skinning his cats and I'll take care of my own kitchen!'

'There's no sense arguing with him, miss,' the small older man interrupted. 'Just like talking to the wind, and besides, he's only having you on. My cat's broken down and won't be working for at least a week, and when he asked me to come give you a hand, he never said one word about being a bodyguard.'

One look at Grey's face confirmed the truth of the statement, although he immediately brushed it aside by stating, 'Well, I'm saying it now. You're to keep an eye on her, Baldy, and I mean that. A cook like this one is too valuable to take any chances with.'

'Fine for you to say, but I know more about kitchens

than you do, and I've no wish to stay in one where I'm not wanted,' Baldy replied with such a downcast expression that Kelly relented instantly.

'Oh, it isn't that at all,' she assured him. 'I really would like to have you, honestly. It's just that . . .'

'It's just that she's a bit too liberated for her own good,' Grey interrupted.

'Which is just about the kind of chauvinistic thing I'd expect you to say,' Kelly snapped. 'I should have expected you to object to any woman who didn't grovel at your feet.'

'See what I mean?' he grinned. 'You watch her, Baldy, or next thing she'll be after your job.'

'I couldn't do it and you know it,' Kelly replied, her face red with anger. Then she turned to Baldy. 'But I promise you, if you skin a cat for me, I'll cook it and feed it to *him*!'

She didn't understand the howls of laughter that erupted from both men at that response, until Grey, tears streaming down his cheeks, managed to catch enough breath to answer her.

'A cat-skinner, my dear Kelly, is a bulldozer operator,' he gasped. 'And I don't think even your immense talents could make a palatable meal from a bulldozer, although I don't doubt you'd probably give it a try.'

At her look of mingled chagrin and embarrassment, he only laughed harder, and when Kelly turned away towards the sanctity of her kitchen, he went the other way, still laughing as he walked through the door.

'You can't say you didn't deserve that one, miss,' said a voice behind her, and Kelly turned to see Baldy, his face screwed into a gargoyle ugliness but his eyes so filled with genuine compassion she could have hugged him.

'He makes me so mad I could spit!' she replied. 'I've never met such an infuriating man in my entire life, and when I think of some of the chefs I've known, that's saying a very great deal indeed.'

'Ah, he can be maddening all right,' the little man

agreed. 'Especially when you reckon he's got a temper as quick as I imagine yours is. But he's a good man for all that, and at least he doesn't ever carry a grudge. When I think of some of the battles we used to have . . .'

Baldy's voice droned on and on as Kelly treated herself to the luxury of a pot of tea, which he shared, but she hardly listened to what he was saying because she was lost in her own thoughts.

So Grey Scofield didn't carry a grudge. It was something on which Kelly had always prided herself, having been forced to learn control of her own fiery temper, but after the past day's encounters with Grey, she was busily vowing that she would *learn* to hold a grudge. And when she finally got her revenge . . .

'What's that you just said?' she blurted out, startling Baldy so badly he almost dropped his cup.

'What? Oh, I was recalling the first time—the last time, as well—that I tried to feed Grey spinach,' he replied with a reminiscent smile. 'You may think you've seen him being hostile, but I figured that day I'd be out on my . . . tail . . . in the snow,' he chuckled. 'And he said if I ever tried it again I would be, too.'

'So he doesn't like spinach,' Kelly mused aloud, unaware she was speaking more to herself than to Baldy. The idea that sprang forth needed little nourishing; it emerged in full bloom.

'Actually, maybe I have been letting him get to me, just a bit,' she admitted with an encouraging smile. 'And since it's probably my fault, perhaps I'd better not make things worse by inadvertently cooking things he hates. You'll have to advise me, Mr Swan. Just what are Mr Scofield's particular dislikes in food?'

'I'd be happier if you'd just call me Baldy,' he replied, 'and happier yet if you'd forget what I think you're thinking, although I think you won't.'

'But certainly it would make things easier all round if I

took pains to avoid Mr Scofield's particular dislikes?' Kelly protested. 'After all, he *is* the boss.'

'He is that,' Baldy agreed, 'and let me tell you, miss, he isn't known as the grey wolf for nothing. And what *you're* thinking is something no sane person would even contemplate.'

'All I want to do is avoid trouble in future,' she said, 'so I can't quite see what you're getting at.'

'You know very well what I'm getting at,' the tiny old man muttered with a grimace. 'But I can see you're not going to admit it, which is about what I'd expect. Okay, I'll help you, or at least that's *my* excuse. I just hope I never really need it. As of this moment, my girl, I claim total ignorance of what I suspect you're planning. But let me warn you: if the . . . er . . . if the proverbial fan gets hit, it'll be entirely on your head. I want your promise of that.'

'Baldy, you're a dear,' Kelly replied with a melting smile. 'And I just don't see how you could do anything else, since I've asked you, but tell me every single thing you know about Grey Scofield's taste in food.'

He shook his head sadly. 'Well, I just hope I'm back cat-skinning before the war starts,' he muttered with a cautious expression. 'And as for you, my girl, just you remember the old grey wolf has teeth.'

'I certainly shall,' Kelly replied determinedly. 'But let us not forget that it's the fox who has the reputation for cunning.'

During the next two days Kelly was forced, despite her aversion to Grey Scofield, to mentally thank him several times a day for lending her Baldy Swan. The diminutive old reprobate was like a ray of sunshine in the overworked cookhouse, helping Kelly a great deal indeed and filling her occasional idle moments with a vivid store of interesting and delightful stories.

He got along splendidly with both women, showed himself to be a worthy colleague in the kitchen, and if he was really being Kelly's bodyguard he did it so unobtrusively that she never even noticed. She was also too busy to notice, since a co-ordinated study of the menus and larder pointed up a considerable need for extensive reorganisation if she was to maintain her reputation as the miracle-maker of the kitchen.

She was honestly sorry when Marcel Leduc got through on the radio-telephone with news that he would be sending her two cooks the next day, and that they both seemed eager, well trained and likely to stay for a considerable period. Kelly knew it was necessary, but she couldn't help feeling she would rather have continued coping as she was with Baldy's help; she had come to have a great affection for the crumpled little cat-skinner.

Still, she couldn't tell Marcel that, so she pretended great pleasure at his news, so much so that she only remembered just in time to get in her request for extra supplies to be sent with the men.

'It's sort of a long list,' she said. 'The first thing, and the most important of all, is spinach, but I also want . . .'

The two cooks turned up early next morning with virtually every item on Kelly's special order list, and she spent most of the day getting them settled in. Fred Griffiths, the new first cook, was a tall, slender man of about thirty whose quiet, decisive attitude and professional approach pleased Kelly a great deal. She knew instinctively she would have no problems at all with him. The new second cook was, on appearances, less impressive. A stout, greying man of about fifty, he conducted himself with the flamboyance of a used car salesman, which Kelly found slightly off-putting at first. His name, he said, was Smith. No Christian name needed. In actual fact his surname was a Ukrainian-based conglomeration of letters that was unpronounceable and virtually unspellable, and he admitted to using it so seldom he could barely spell it himself.

'Smith'll do,' he assured Kelly after spending fifteen minutes laboriously tracing out his tongue-twister name on the myriad forms required for tax and benefit purposes.

'Smith it is, then,' she replied dubiously, and was pleasantly surprised within the next week to find him a highly competent cook and an efficient organiser.

Grey Scofield returned later that same say, and after overhearing a chance remark in the dining room that assured her he would be staying at least four days, Kelly threw her own Operation Wolf Bait into high gear. Somewhat reluctantly, since she would have preferred a few more days to prepare herself mentally before setting out to so deliberately annoy Grey Scofield.

But given much more time, she knew instinctively she would shy away from such a drastic plan, and she managed to convince herself that revenge was not only advisable but necessary if she wasn't to find herself totally subjugated by Grey's forceful personality.

Operation Wolf Bait began with baked beans on toast. Kelly had decided to save the spinach for the *coup de grâce*, but since Baldy's comments indicated baked beans on toast ran a close second to spinach in Grey's list of dislikes, she thought it an appropriate kick-off to the campaign.

It wasn't an auspicious beginning. A minor disaster in the kitchen drew Kelly from the servery before she could catch the look on Grey's face when he drew his portion of the breakfast, and she was kept too busy to check on whether he had eaten it, rejected it, or whatever. Rather disappointing, she thought, and vowed to keep a closer eye on things at dinner that night, when she was serving chicken in a complicated sauce that fairly swarmed with mushrooms.

It was her intention to somehow slop the mushroom sauce over everything on Grey's plate, but she hadn't allowed for her own nervousness. Her trembling fingers came so close to missing the plate entirely that he looked at her with vague surprise and muttered something about working too hard, but he said nothing about being served a dish that he would violently dislike.

Kelly did get some satisfaction from seeing him throw some rather peculiar looks in her direction during dinner, but she had no way of knowing whether they stemmed from his dislike of the food or her own clumsiness. There was no satisfaction in the fact that he cleaned his plate.

She was beginning to despair when during the following two days he uncomplainingly ate heaped servings of cauliflower, brussels sprouts, broccoli, corned beef and cabbage and even sauerkraut. She invariably managed to give him enormous helpings of the foods he disliked, but never by a single word or glance did he reveal that he was annoyed or even mildly upset by her actions.

The final dinner in Operation Wolf Bait was fraught with anxiety for Kelly, and the fact that Grey was last in to dinner did little to assuage her nervousness. He arrived finally, about five minutes later than the rest of the men, and when Kelly had loaded his plate and handed it to him, he gave her one of his slow, gentle grins and handed it back.

'Can I have some more spinach, please?' he asked quietly, and Kelly took the plate without realising she had done so and began spooning on more spinach.

'But ... but you ...' Her voice failed her as she raised her eyes to meet the mocking laughter in his own.

'It was a helluva good try,' he laughed. 'The only thing is, old Baldy hasn't cooked for me in nearly ten years, and my tastes have matured considerably in that time.'

Kelly was speechless. Worse than speechless; her face was so flushed with embarrassment that her freckles virtually disappeared in the blush and she had the awful, frightening suspicion that she was going to burst into tears.

And if he laughed outright, she would, and the knowledge was almost enough to make her flee to the sanctuary of the kitchen, only she was held by those piercing grey eyes, pinned like a butterfly to a collector's board. What could she say? The answer was obvious: nothing.

'If it's any consolation, I still have a morbid aversion to scalloped potatoes,' he said with a wry grin, then turned away and walked into the dining room to join his men.

Kelly took a moment to check that everything was running smoothly in the kitchen, then fled to her trailer and threw herself on the bed, pounding her small fists into the pillows and wishing she could so easily vent her anger on that infuriating Grey Scofield. Her entire revenge had been a total, dismal failure. And worse, she had emerged looking quite the fool and with very little chance of redeeming herself.

It was difficult to sleep that night. She kept reliving those horrid moments, and seeing the mocking look in Grey's eyes as he had put her firmly and properly in her place. And to have the absolute effrontery to admit his aversion to scalloped potatoes . . . it was absolutely maddening!

Maddening, and so tauntingly superior that she spent most of the next day in a flaming temper that nobody in the kitchen missed. Kelly thought up dozens of vengeful comments, many of them outrageously silly, and wound up ordering that scalloped potatoes would be served with dinner. She felt silly once she'd done so, and as the day progressed she began to feel increasingly small and petty.

'I just can't do it,' she muttered aloud about ten minutes before the dinner gong. 'I . . . can't!'

The next few minutes was a bit of a scramble, but when Grey sauntered into the servery to collect his meal, she was unexpectedly pleased to be able to bypass the scalloped potatoes and give him the hash-browns she had personally prepared at the last minute.

'Thank you, Kelly. That was very nice of you to take such trouble,' he said with a perfectly straight face and without a hint of mockery in his eyes.

Kelly, barely able to contain her shyness after spending considerable effort to put on a brave face for the occasion, could have wept. Even in victory, he showed his superiority, and she felt more petty than before. For the first time since her arrival at Kakwa camp, she began to seriously doubt the wisdom of trying to continue managing the catering of any camp where Grey Scofield held the reins of control.

I hate him, I hate him, I hate him! she told herself silently in bed that night, knowing the lie as she said it but unable to admit that knowledge even to herself.

Grey's absence at breakfast next morning did even less to improve Kelly's humour, especially when old Baldy remarked that the camp boss had left at first light to drive into Grande Prairie. The fact that Grey hadn't even mentioned it to her, though he must have known it was her day to drive into the city for supplies, nagged at Kelly throughout the long drive north. Of course it was none of her business what he did, but it would have been nice, she thought, if they could have at least arranged to meet somewhere for coffee, or lunch, or something!

By the time she reached Grande Prairie and threaded her cautious way through the masses of heavy truck traffic to the hospital, she was in such a blue funk herself that she wondered briefly if she should visit her father at all in such a mood. But of course she had to visit him, since he would have been expecting her, she reasoned, and indeed he was.

'You look absolutely wonderful,' he grinned when Kelly walked softly into his hospital room. 'Looks like the bush agrees with you, which shouldn't really surprise me, I guess. But after what Grey said about you working so hard, I expected you to be looking all pale and peaked.'

'He said what?' Kelly immediately feared the worst, and she awaited her father's report with twinges of conscience that made her overly apprehensive.

'He said you've been working like a Trojan,' Geoff

Barnes replied with a grin, 'and that the results have been nothing short of miraculous.'

He laughed aloud at Kelly's look of bewilderment. 'It looks like you've done everything right,' he said. 'Grey's been singing your praises to the skies. He thinks you're the greatest thing since sliced bread.'

'I don't believe it,' Kelly replied in a stunned voice. 'Practically all we've done since I got there is fight, and after ... just when was he being so complimentary, anyway?'

'About half an hour ago, the last time. But he's dropped in a couple of times since you moved south, just to reassure me everything was okay, I guess. Just as well, since you've obviously been too busy to make the trip.'

Her father's voice held a slightly reproving note that tugged at Kelly's emotions. It had only been just over a week, but he was right, she had been too busy even to feel guilty about not making the drive in to see him.

'Now don't go feeling guilty about it,' Geoff Barnes said with a grin. 'I know you've been too busy and I know why. And I've already had words with Marcel about those two drunken cooks he hired when I took sick. You've done a splendid job, Kelly, but now that you have everything under control I just hope the weather holds good so you can be sure of getting up here every few days for a visit. I'm getting awfully sick of this hospital.'

Kelly promised faithfully to try and get up at least twice a week, and for the rest of their visit they talked about the work she was doing and the people at the camp.

Geoff Barnes admitted that Grey seemed to be overreacting just a bit about Kelly's need for protection, but he was adamant that she should honour Grey's wishes in the matter. 'It's far better to be safe than sorry in this case,' he said. 'And while it may seem a bit restrictive, you should be flattered that Grey thinks enough of you to be so careful.'

'He's only thinking of his stomach,' she retorted. 'And he

is over-reacting. I've got to know most of the men, well . . . reasonably well anyway, and I'm positive in my own mind there isn't a single one of them that would even think of harming me.'

'Fair enough, but I've spent a lifetime in these camps, and let me tell you, my girl, there are some strange characters on some of these crews. You can argue with Grey if you like, but he's got my support in this and I've told him so.'

'Thanks a lot,' Kelly said tartly. 'That's all I need is for you to give him carte blanche authority over my private life, not that I've got much time for any private life anyway, but it's the principle of the thing.'

'You couldn't be in better hands,' her father replied calmly. 'Once I'm back on my feet it'll be different, but until then I'm just happy that Grey was willing to take on the responsibility.'

'But I don't want to be his responsibility,' she cried. 'I'm twenty-four years old, Father. I'm not a child and I resent him thinking I am and treating me like one. And really I think it's unfair of you to put me in such a position.'

'Gently with the temper, Kelly. I'm supposed to be a sick man,' her father replied. 'And as for Grey treating you like a child, I got the distinct impression from him that he thinks of you as anything but a child, for whatever consolation that is.'

'None whatsoever! He's the most autocratic, chauvinistic man I've ever met,' Kelly snapped.

'Are you just angry because your little scheme failed, or is it because you're falling for him a bit yourself?' her father replied with a knowing grin.

'Oh. How did you . . . you know?' Kelly stammered. The nerve of Grey Schofield to tell her father about that . . . that horrendous, dismal failure of a revenge! She was first angry, then shyly contrite as her father laughed out loud.

'Of course he told me,' Geoff Barnes laughed. 'He thought it was tremendously funny. And so do I—but only because he did.' His voice took on a warning note. 'In actual fact, it was extremely petty of you, Kelly, and I'm not amused by that. I would never have thought you to be a vindictive person.'

'And I'm not, usually,' she sighed. 'But Grey Scofield just gets my hackles up like nobody I've ever met. And what's worse, he never seems to even have to try. It just happens. But you're right, it was petty, and I'm sorry and I shall try not to blot my copybook again. But he just makes me so angry . . .'

'That's probably because you have no sense of humour,' drawled a gravelly voice from the doorway. 'But I'll make it up to you by buying you lunch.'

Kelly turned with a startled cry to find Grey Scofield lounging carelessly against the door jamb, his eyes wrinkled with wry amusement at her surprise. How long had he been there, she wondered immediately, and worse, how much had he heard?

Dressed in clean khaki shirt and trousers, with the shirt sleeves rolled above his powerful forearms and the front undone to reveal a thatch of dark chest hair, Grey seemed to exude an air of intense masculinity and a youthfulness that belied his silver hair. His mouth was quirked in a mocking half-smile and his grey eyes clearly awaited Kelly's response to the invitation.

'I'm sorry, but I'll be too busy to take time for lunch,' she finally blurted after an over-long delay that fooled neither Grey nor her father.

'Suit yourself,' he said with a shrug, revealing that he hadn't expected her to accept in the first place.

Kelly, for some reason she couldn't work out, was strangely hurt by his abrupt reaction, and immediately after he had spoken briefly to her father and left the room without another word to her, she was wishing she had accepted the invitation.

'You should have,' said Geoff Barnes, as if reading his daughter's mind. 'You'll never get anywhere with Grey Scofield by fighting, I can tell you that right now.'

'I'm not interested in getting anywhere with Mr Scofield, thank you very much,' Kelly replied tartly. 'I would much prefer it if he would just stick to his job and leave me to mine.'

'Well, if that's your story, you stick to it,' her father replied with a grin. Then he immediately changed the subject, and whenever Kelly brought Grey's name into the conversation during the rest of her visit, he adroitly changed the subject again. It was frustrating, but she could hardly insist upon discussing a man in whom she professed no interest at all.

Soon she could tell that the strain of the visit was telling upon her father. He needed to rest, not talk to her, and she withdrew as graciously as she could without making him feel guilty about his weakness. Returning to the downtown shopping area, she began the long and tiring task of filling her supply list.

She was placing the last of the non-perishables into the back of the truck when a strangely familiar voice called to her, and she turned to meet the approach of Marcel Leduc, striding across the parking lot with a broad smile on his handsome face.

'Your dad said I'd likely find you here,' he said with a grin. 'And you've finished just in time for lunch, so let's be off.'

It wasn't the most favourable suggestion; Kelly could have thought of more enjoyable companions. She didn't entirely trust Marcel and she didn't really like him much, though she had no solid reason for either reaction.

But she also had no valid reason for refusing him, and when he gently and gallantly took her arm, she hesitated only for an instant before flashing him a broad smile of acceptance.

As they approached Marcel's chosen restaurant, already starting to fill with the lunch-time trade, Kelly had a brief twinge of regret. She could have been lunching with Grey Scofield, except for her own perverseness, she thought, and then was immediately angry with herself for thinking of it. Until they were seated at a remote corner table and she looked up to see that familiar silver hair reflected in a mirror on the opposite wall.

Her first response was to bow her head; it would be the height of embarrassment if Grey were to find her lunching with somebody else after refusing his invitation. But after a moment she realised that Marcel's presence gave her a perfect excuse, even if she hadn't mentioned it at the time Grey had asked her to lunch.

Besides, his back was to her in the mirror, and she found a certain smug satisfaction in being able to watch him without his knowledge. She was enjoying that somewhat illicit pleasure when an audible hush fell over the restaurant, which was mostly filled with roughly-dressed bush workers and oilmen. The image in the mirror rose to its feet, and Kelly turned to view the arrival of the most stunning blonde she had seen since leaving England.

Tall, perhaps five foot seven without the three-inch heels that gave added grace to slender, shapely legs, the girl had shag-cut, flowing hair of such a light blondeness that it could only be natural. And she was extraordinarily beautiful, with classic features and large blue-green eyes. She wore a close-fitting white outfit that outlined every detail of a magnificent figure, and Kelly was immediately jealous of the response this creature spurred from every single man in the room.

'Grey darling!' the blonde trilled in a husky, throaty voice. 'I'm so sorry I'm late. But you don't really mind, do you?'

Kelly couldn't hear the muted response as Grey Scofield seated his lovely companion, but she felt the sigh of disappointment that swept the room as the blonde was seated where most of the men could no longer admire her long legs. Angered as much by her own jealousy as anything else, Kelly turned her attention back to her meal, but it had lost its allure, and she looked up to find Marcel Leduc's eyes roving past her to complete his own assessment of the statuesque blonde.

His attention was so rapt that Kelly's resentment grew dangerously violent, and she had to restrain the impulse to kick him under the table. Instead, she waved her hand in a childish gesture beneath his nose, saying, 'Hey! Remember me?'

'Remember you? But it was you that I was thinking of,' he lied blandly, unaware of her knowledge, via the mirror, of where his attention had actually been directed.

For the balance of the meal, however, he was typically Gallic in his attentions to Kelly, paying her outrageous compliments throughout a seemingly innocent conversation that delved quite deeply into her intentions about the business and her own place in the future scheme of things. Kelly wasn't fooled for a moment; she had already decided that her presence might prove difficult for Marcel's future plans, and she sensed that he rather resented her arrival in a business that had otherwise promised him a lucrative and independent future.

Marcel was aiming for a full partnership, she knew, and indeed had been taken into her father's business with that in mind, since Geoff Barnes had only half believed in Kelly's own determination to make a new life in Canada. But Kelly was also aware of Marcel's interest in her as a woman, an interest that had taken a severe nose-dive with the arrival of the blonde vision across the room.

When they had finished lunch, Kelly followed Marcel to the reception desk and the doorway, thinking as she did so that it was fortunate Grey Scofield's attentions were fully diverted. He would never notice her in any event, since her tiny figure in jeans and a light cotton blouse didn't stand out with anything like the flamboyance of his blonde companion.

She had reckoned without the mirrors, however, and even as she turned towards the doorway after Marcel had paid the bill, she found herself meeting Grey Scofield's eyes as she looked into the mirror by the door and found it reflecting his image in yet another mirror across the room.

One dark eyebrow raised in a scornful, or was it a mocking gesture of acknowledgment? Kelly didn't wait to find out. She turned and dashed through the door without revealing that she had seen Grey, breathing quickly as she reached the sanctuary of the busy street outside.

But her day was entirely spoiled by the encounter, and she found herself lying desperately to get rid of Marcel as quickly as possible, then scurrying around the supermarkets to pick up her perishable groceries and get herself out of town as quickly as she could.

All the long way back to Kakwa camp, she kept seeing those grey eyes, mocking her, laughing at her, tormenting her. And worse, she kept wondering as she guided the large truck over the rough gravel track, if Grey had made his date with the gorgeous blonde after he had asked Kelly herself to lunch, or before.

It was a question she didn't enjoy facing at all, but she couldn't get it out of her mind. When he didn't show up for dinner that night, she lay awake later in her trailer, listening in vain for the sound of his arriving truck and wondering how he and the blonde were spending the evening. She fell asleep, finally, without knowing if he had even come back to camp that night.

CHAPTER FOUR

By the time Grey Scofield returned to camp, just barely in
time to sit in at the tag end of breakfast, Kelly had firmly
decided she couldn't care less about his associations with
the mysterious blonde or indeed any other woman. It
wasn't her business, and since she didn't think much of him
anyway, it was patently ridiculous to let him bother her no
matter what he chose to do.

With her new cooks well under control, she was treating
herself to the unaccustomed luxury of a breakfast prepared
by somebody else, and when Grey arrived she was seated
alone at a small table in the corner of the dining hall.

She had noticed several of the men, especially the young
blond giant she had noticed the first day of her arrival,
working to build up the courage to join her, but she was
initially determined to maintain the cool distance she had
thought best to keep away from any kind of man trouble in
the camp. Much as she detested Grey's insinuations about
possible problems, she knew in her heart that he was
actually right, and she was determined to give him no
cause for complaint on that score, at least.

But when the tall, grey-eyed man walked into the dining
room, the cat-that-ate-the-canary look on his face brought
an abrupt surge of spitefulness rushing through her, and
just for an instant she wished she had been surrounded by
his men when the camp boss arrived.

She wished it even more when Grey loaded his breakfast
tray and coolly strode over to sling himself into a chair
across from her without so much as a thought about
whether she might have preferred to breakfast alone. Had
she been closer to being finished, Kelly might have been

able to conceive an escape, but by the time she thought of that, it was far too late.

'Morning,' he grinned cheerfully, bold grey eyes roving across her face in undisguised appraisal.

For just an instant, she couldn't help but think of the obvious comparisons between herself and the gorgeous blonde Grey had lunched with the day before, and she very nearly flushed at her own vulnerability. Then she steeled herself to return his greeting as casually as possible, and without consciously planning it, added: 'You look as if you had a good night.'

There was a flash of something in his eyes, a flash that flickered so quickly she couldn't tell if it was anger, amusement or just what. A tiny grin quirked up the corner of his strong, passionate mouth before he replied.

'I did, Miss Barnes. I surely did,' he said quietly, and as he returned his attention to the food before him, she caught another glimmer of what had to be laughter in his eyes.

Kelly fumed inwardly. How dare he laugh at her! she thought. Flaunting his blonde companion like a trophy before her. What did she care who he spent his nights with?

'I was only being polite,' she said quite unnecessarily, and was rewarded with another half-grin.

'Of course,' he said calmly.

'Well, I was!'

'Okay,' he said, shrugging as if to rid himself of an annoying mosquito or fly.

Kelly felt increasingly foolish, unable to control her own thoughts and emotions, or—worse—her tongue. She knew that no matter what she said, it would only lead her deeper into trouble, but she couldn't gracefully back away. Damn the man, she thought. It wasn't right that he should have such an effect upon her, especially when she didn't even like him.

Nonetheless, she didn't avoid the opportunity as he ate to study his strong, muscular wrists and hands, the set of his powerful neck, where curling black hair rolled up out of the neckline of his khaki shirt. He was a handsome devil, she had to admit, although not in any really conventional fashion. The silvery hair was vivid against his deep-tanned face, and his piercing eyes even more so as he looked up to catch her studying him.

'You want to buy it, or are you just looking?' he asked with a wry grin.

'I . . . I was just thinking that some women would pay a healthy price at the hairdresser to achieve the colour you've got naturally,' Kelly replied lamely.

'Indeed? But how do you know it's natural?' he replied, then laughed aloud at her flushed response.

'You . . . you just don't strike me as the type to have it dyed,' she replied, struggling to hold her temper. She could almost feel the solidifying atmosphere around them as the other men gradually became aware of the conflicting confrontation.

'Oh,' Grey replied with one sooty eyebrow raised in query. 'And just what type *do* I strike you as?'

'No type that interests me,' she flared back, angered at having so neatly trapped herself. Grabbing up her tray, oblivious to the half-full plate and coffee-cup, she strode back towards the kitchen with her back rigid in anger, ignoring the whistle that followed her perky manoeuvre and knowing as she did so that it wouldn't have been Grey Scofield who did the whistling. That, she decided, certainly wouldn't fit his style.

By lunchtime she had regained her composure, assisted by finding that her kitchen duties could now be reduced to a purely supervisory role and that she could devote some time to the administrative aspects of her work. She took only a light snack for lunch, especially compared to the full-scale meals the men of the camp seemed to require, and she was gone from the kitchen area when, or if, Grey had his midday meal.

At dinner that evening she chose to stay in the kitchen, helping out where she was needed, and it wasn't until the meal was virtually over that she realised Grey hadn't shown up at all. Nor did he arrive for breakfast the following morning, or all of that day either, and by dinner time she was edgy and sharp with everyone, despite knowing her real anger was with herself for allowing the tall grey-haired man to affect her so strongly.

Even during her drive into Grande Prairie the following morning, she kept finding her mind drifting to re-focus into the strength of Grey's profile, or the quirk of his vivid mouth, and once, the angering sight of him sitting with his lovely blonde companion in the restaurant.

There was little actual business to be done on this trip to town. Kelly had some correspondence to mail, a few things to check up on, but mostly she was just going in to visit her father and check on his progress. She arrived in Grande Prairie before the shops were even open, having left Kakwa camp shortly after the midsummer dawn and without having waited for breakfast. Even that early, however, the bustling traffic made it difficult to find a parking space downtown.

Once she had the heavy pick-up truck parked, she sat for a moment and simply watched the world go by, all of it seemingly comprised of rough-hewn oil workers in their khaki or olive-green shirts and trousers, clumping heavily in sturdy, lace-up work boots or high-heeled riding boots. Headgear ranged from baseball caps with long, grease-stained peaks to fancy, expensive cowboy hats in a multitude of colours.

A boom town! Difficult indeed to imagine that Grande Prairie, as one of Canada's most northerly towns, was on virtually the same fifty-five-plus degrees—as Moscow and the vast wilderness of Siberia.

A town where waitresses and barmaids made unbelievably huge salaries, and where the unemployment problem was created not by a lack of jobs, but by a lack of somewhere for people to live. There were more jobs than people, and during summer more people than the existing accommodation could hold. There was a growing number of itinerant workers living just outside the city in tents because the housing boom couldn't keep up with the demand for accommodation.

To Kelly's eyes it was like a whole new world, so vibrant, so totally alive despite the squalor of trucks that were filthy with mud and grease because the time to clean them simply couldn't be spared, despite the throngs of loud, rough, vigorous men on the footpaths and the dense traffic on the streets. It was like nothing she had ever seen in her life, and she was half afraid to leave the safety of her own vehicle and throw herself into the throngs on the street—yet equally half afraid not to, for fear of missing something.

There was a bustle and an excitement that was contagious, for some reason even more so now than during her first few days in the city, when she had watched the crowds without realising how fortunate she had been in arriving without notice to find her father's small but well-stocked home awaiting her.

Hospital visiting hours wouldn't start for some time, so she strolled the streets downtown, peering excitedly into shop windows, and once they opened, into the fascinating interiors of the shops themselves. She had to stand in line for ten minutes at one café just to get a cup of tea, but even that delay was filled with wonderment at the mixture of accents and voices that boomed through the small café.

Polish, Ukrainian, French-Canadian, the occasional nasal twang that denoted an American, the soft patois of the native Metis people, those of mixed Indian and white blood whose language could be anything from almost-French to one of several Indian dialects. It was a rich, heady mixture that took in most of the European accents and racial types.

Geoff Barnes, to Kelly's delight, seemed much improved from her visit only days before, and though he spoke sadly of yet another fortnight in the hospital and a long period of convalescence after that, she was heartened by his improved colour and obvious return to something like the father she remembered.

He was, however, somewhat less than equally pleased at her own appearance.

'It's not much wonder you're having trouble with Grey Scofield if you run around dressed like that,' he muttered with a disparaging glance over her checked shirt and jeans. 'Just because you're living out in the bush it doesn't mean you have to dress like one of the boys as well.'

He brushed aside her protestations about the folly of wearing a fancy dress to drive more than a hundred miles to town over questionable roads in a pick-up truck.

'Ridiculous! You've got the house here—go out and buy some decent clothes this afternoon and put them on there. In fact, stay over tonight while you're at it . . . see a show or something. And when you come back to see me this afternoon, I want you looking like my daughter, not somebody's teenage son.'

She would have been angry with him, except for the memory of a lovely little dress she had noticed in one shop window that morning. It was a pale green, ideally suited to her slender, diminutive figure, and ideal also for getting dressed up to go out in the evening without looking far too overdressed in a town where half the dining-out crowd in a restaurant were dressed up and the rest were in working gear.

'Buy it!' her father ordered at her tenuous mention of the garment. 'In fact buy half a dozen of them for all I care. Goodness, girl. We can afford it, you know.'

He grinned engagingly, then a slight spasm of pain crossed his face and Kelly realised she had stayed too long; he was tired.

'Oh, all right,' she consented. 'I'll buy out Grande Prairie if it'll make you happy. And I promise to look more like a girl when I come this afternoon. Or would you like me to give that a miss? You look very tired all of a sudden.'

'No way,' her father denied stoutly. 'I'll be fine by this afternoon, and even better to see you looking civilised for a change. Now off you go.'

She went. And several hours later she was wheeling the truck into a parking space near her father's house, idly wondering why even the city's residential streets should be clogged with vehicles.

She needed three trips to unload the bags and boxes of clothes she had purchased since leaving the hospital. In addition to the pale green dress, she had found four other suitable dresses, two pant suits and various other items of clothing that suited her admirably. Perhaps her favourite, however, was a gay green-and-white gingham frock with a peasant neckline and flowing, carefree lines that accentuated her femininity without drawing undue attention to her youthful size.

When she finally finished unloading her purchases on to the living room sofa, it was the gingham she opened first, intending to wear it to visit her father that afternoon.

But with two hours before the visiting time, she was suddenly struck by her own tiredness, and after taking all her purchases into the bedroom she had used previously, she stacked them on a wardrobe and laid herself down on the bed with the idea of grabbing just a quick nap.

She slept fitfully, her rest punctuated by a series of flickering images, half-formed and vague, of wild animals hunting in the forest. Where she herself fitted into the dream, she never did figure out, but Grey Scofield was there as the gaunt, wild leader of a wolf pack, moving with a free, almost ghostly ease of movement that was both terrifying and irresistible.

Even in the dream, one of those vague types that occur

only in the half-world between sleep and wakefulness, Kelly was aware that she should have been there, should have been prancing in a red fox pelt far ahead of the wolf pack, using cunning and vixen know-how to keep herself safe. But although she saw the dream through the eyes of a watcher, she could not see herself at all.

Marcel Leduc was there; he pranced behind the leader in a reddish-brown pelt that matched the hair of the living man. The eyes of the reddish wolf were those of the French-Canadian, though his face was never clear.

And suddenly, to the amazement and fearful surprise of Kelly as the dream-watcher, the blonde vision from the restaurant was there also, a lithe, graceful she-wolf with a coat so stunningly white-blonde it gleamed like sun-fire, and ice-blue eyes that seemed to see Kelly watching her.

The she-wolf led the grey leader into a dance of leaping, joyful pre-mating, and when her eyes weren't locked with his, leading him on, they flashed like mocking beacons, derisive and laughing at Kelly. The two animals ran and bounded and turned back upon themselves like the flickering of an open fire, the grey wolf unheedful of everything in his quest for the female, but the pale, white-blonde one clearly aware of the watcher and mocking her.

They gambolled through the meadows, into and out of huge, park-like timber, and finally to the edge of a high, glass-clear mountain river that Kelly's dream mind recognised as the Kakwa River above the falls. Smirking, the she-wolf drew her follower into the crystal, sparkling waters, swimming with powerful movements downstream to where the waters sped over the high rim of the bedrock, past the enormous cave beneath the waterfall's crest, to thunder in a cacophony of spray on the rocks below.

And where the dream had been silent, it suddenly took on noise and dimension as the gaunt grey wolf gave himself to the pull of the current, allowing the river to carry him downstream to his pale feminine counterpart, or to the falls themselves.

Kelly seemed rooted, unable to follow the descent except in her vision, and this outraged her. Throughout the earlier part of the dream her third-person status had followed the wolves like a shadow, but now she was rooted in one spot, able only to watch as the two figures dwindled in size on their downstream journey.

Her sight dimmed by distance, she saw the blonde figure emerge from the rushing, sun-drenched waters, shake like a dog and then suddenly rear itself erect in a dramatic resumption of human form. But the other figure, the grey one, was captivated by the torrent, and she heard a yodelling howl as it was dragged towards the brink of the falls amid the roaring hiss of the river.

Again that awesome howl, this time taking on a note of desperation as the water surged louder . . .

Kelly's eyes snapped open, suddenly wide awake as she realised the yodel—and indeed the hiss of falling water—was more real than dream. The sound came again, this time a definite yodel against the noise of the shower in the bathroom next door, and she flung herself from the bed in a single scurrying motion.

Her clothes lay where she had laid them, and without thinking much about it she grabbed up the gingham dress and slipped it over her bare shoulders as she stalked towards the bedroom door, her bare feet soundless on the carpet. The bathroom door was shut, and for the moment she ignored it as she scurried to the kitchen and grabbed up the first weapon she could find, the carving knife.

It never occurred to her to take the course of common sense—straight out the front door and into the relative safety of the street. Indeed, she would wonder later at whatever devil possessed her to result in five foot three of redhaired girl sneaking up on the closed bathroom like an Indian on the warpath.

She was almost there, moving inch by inch as she tried to bolster her nerve, when she suddenly realised that the noise of the shower had ceased.

Kelly stopped, one foot in the air and the knife poised in her hand, but even as her mind tried to assimilate this new circumstance, the bathroom door opened.

'What the hell are you playing at?' The voice took on a rising note at the end of the question, but once glance at the pale eyes told her that it wasn't a note of fear.

Indeed, Grey Scofield's eyes held only a heaping measure of bewilderment as he stood, casual yet poised for motion if it should be necessary, naked to the towel that encircled his trim, muscular waist. His generous mouth was quirked in a half-grin, and his eyes sparkled beneath the mop of curly, still-wet hair that dripped tiny sparkles of water on to his broad shoulders.

Nowhere was there the slightest indication that he found it unusual to emerge from the shower to be confronted by a knife-wielding redhead, and his total calmness struck at Kelly like a physical blow.

She herself was anything but calm. The surprise of finding her unexpected visitor was Grey Scofield was enough in itself to make her speechless, but the sight of that immensely masculine form so close—and so close to nakedness—only made things worse.

'Wha . . . what are you doing here?' she finally stammered, putting down her upraised foot and dropping her hands to her sides as if no longer aware of the foot-long knife in her hand.

Grey's eyes flashed with subdued laughter. 'Well, I could be going to a Roman tea-party,' he grinned. 'Or . . .' with a significant look at the knife Kelly still held '. . . I could be preparing myself to be a virgin sacrifice. But actually I was just taking a shower.'

'That's not what I meant and you know it,' she snapped, her anger rising to replace the confusion inside her. 'What are you doing here, in my father's house?'

'I thought I just answered that,' he replied calmly. 'But I suppose you want to know what right I have to be taking a shower in your father's house? Simple, actually. Since there's such a shortage of accommodation in town, we agreed it would be easiest all round. He uses my house when he's in Calgary, if that helps explain anything to you.'

'So you just come and go as you please, without asking permission or anything?' Kelly knew the answer before she asked, but she simply had to say *something* in the face of her growing nervousness of this man.

'Well, I was going to ask your permission,' he replied with a wicked grin, 'but you looked so peaceable, sleeping, that I didn't have the . . .'

'You . . . you Peeping Tom!' Kelly burst out, her freckles disappearing in the flush that rose from her throat at the thought of Grey Scofield looking in on her asleep, wearing only her gauze-thin panties.

'Make up your mind,' he laughed. 'It was either that or be rude. And I can assure you I didn't make a great production of looking you over; I've seen half-naked women before.' He paused, and then: '. . . although seldom any quite as attractive as you, if that helps.'

'It does not!' Kelly's embarrassment had turned quickly, congealing to a white-hot, blazing anger, and her fingers tightened on the handle of the carving knife as if she wanted nothing more than to carve out his laughing, sneaky eyes. Which wasn't far from true, she knew.

Grey glanced at where her knuckles showed white on the knife hasp, and he shook his head sadly. The laughter stayed in his eyes, however, when he spoke.

'All right, I apologise. Although why, I really don't know.' He glanced down at the knife. 'And now, unless you're honestly planning roast Scofield for dinner tonight, why don't you put that thing away and put the coffee on. I'll join you as soon as I'm dressed.'

'You can make your own damned coffee!' she flared. 'And your own dinner as well.'

'Have it your way,' he shrugged. 'But I am going to get dressed, if you don't mind.' And without another glance at the knife, he shouldered his way past her and disappeared into the house's second bedroom, padding wolf-like on his bare feet.

When the door closed behind him, Kelly closed her eyes and shuddered back a scream of absolute frustration, her entire body trembling with the urge to throw something at him. Then she returned the knife to the kitchen and fled to her own room.

The ticking of the bedside clock was an incessant aggravation as Kelly sat on the edge of the bed, her mind busily and fruitlessly trying to analyse her reactions to Grey Scofield. A hateful man! His dominant masculinity and her total inability to fluster him in any way only made his presence impossible for her to ignore, and she resented that fact as well.

Closing her eyes, she tried to shut out the sight of him along with the memory of her weird dream, but her mind insisted on conjuring up the vision of his massive, muscular chest and shoulders, and the trim, taut stomach above the towel. And those horrid, mocking, all-seeing eyes . . .

Finally the clock gave her no option. If she was to visit her father again she couldn't hide in the room any longer. She slipped into the adjoining bathroom only long enough to tidy her hair, trying vainly to shut her nostrils against the heady scent of man that seemed to pervade the still-steamy room. Then she swept up her handbag, straightened her shoulders and walked quickly towards the living room and the front door.

'Coffee's made, if you want some,' Grey's voice growled from where he sat in a large easy-chair. Dressed in a dark business suit, the white shirt gleaming against the depth of his tan, he rose lightly to his feet as she entered the room and seemed to tower over her like a living mountain.

'No ... no, thank you,' she said. 'I'm going to visit Father and I'm late already.'

'Okay,' he shrugged as if it didn't matter to him at all. 'You staying over tonight?'

'Stay the night? With you here? I should certainly hope not!' Kelly thought, not realising she had thought out loud until his rude laugh erupted like a gunshot in the room.

'I wasn't planning to stay over myself,' he said with a smile. 'But I had hoped to be able to buy you dinner. Should have known better, I suppose.'

'You certainly should,' Kelly replied with a primness that almost made her giggle. The humour of the entire situation had suddenly dawned on her, but she was determined not to let him realise that.

'Well, if you change your mind I'll be here between six and seven,' he said. 'After seven the house is yours, and I can assure you there'll be no nocturnal visits from me, at least. But Leduc's in town, and I'd better warn you that he uses the house too, so be careful how you wave that carving knife around or your dad'll be looking for a new second-in-command.'

Kelly was staggered by the information. How many people, she wondered, were likely to use her father's house as a convenient hotel when they were in town? And worse, why hadn't anybody so much as mentioned it to her?

'Only the two of us,' said Grey as if reading her mind. 'And your dad probably would have mentioned it, except that neither Leduc or I do much more than just clean up here and sort of keep an eye on the place. There are ... other places to sleep, as a general rule.'

The innuendo was thinly veiled, and for some reason it refuelled Kelly's anger about the thing.

'I wonder why your girl-friends won't let you have a shower there as well,' she said over-sweetly. 'Or don't you pay them enough?'

And as Grey's eyes blazed with sudden anger, Kelly

strode through the front door and slammed it angrily behind her. She walked down the sidewalk to the street, resisting the urge to turn and stick out her tongue at him. He was watching her; she could feel it like a rifle sighted between her shoulder-blades. And by the time she had driven through the afternoon streets to the hospital, she was already regretting her words as having been impetuously childish and provocative.

Her father wasn't the only one to appreciate her new dress, Kelly found when she arrived at the hospital. But it was the gleam of satisfaction in Geoff Barnes' eyes that pleased her best, rather than the low whistle of appreciation that issued from Marcel Leduc.

The French-Canadian murmured several rather bawdy compliments in his own language before suddenly remembering that Kelly would understand them, whereupon he had the good grace to flush slightly, but it didn't stop him from insisting that they should celebrate her visit to town by going to dinner.

'I must be going back to Peace River straight away afterwards,' he said, as if reading her mind as she thought of sharing the house with him, and Kelly agreed on the dinner date despite a cautious voice inside her shouting loud warnings. Still, she thought, Grey Scofield had said he wouldn't be staying the night, and it was her father's house after all.

'You'll want to clean up and change, of course,' she told Marcel, who looked almost surprised at having been accepted. 'Why not stop by the house at, say, six o'clock? We'll have a drink before dinner, eat early, and you can still make it to Peace River at something like a reasonable hour.'

'*Bien*,' he replied, then excused himself to go and finish his day's business. Kelly spent a few minutes with her father, outlining her plan to stay overnight and get an early start for the camp in the morning. She thought of mentioning her chagrin at not being informed about the apparent house-sharing arrangement, then decided against it after looking at how tired he seemed.

Instead, she went straight home from the hospital and brewed up a pot of tea. Changing back to her jeans and work blouse, she sat in the kitchen and sipped at the brew as she contemplated the reactions when Marcel and Grey found themselves together in the house later that evening.

Just before six, she changed into the pale green dress she had bought, adding a touch of perfume from her handbag and idly wishing she had brought along some proper jewellery. Her watch, with its serviceable leather strap, would be staying at home for certain, and she could only be grateful that pierced ears ensured the minimum tiny gold hoops she wore all the time.

Grey was the first to arrive, and Kelly forced herself to be hostess-like and pleasant to him, seating him comfortably in the big easy-chair and even bringing him the Scotch and soda he warily requested at her insistence.

No mention of the day's earlier encounter; they engaged in absurdly trivial small talk for the ten minutes it took before Marcel Leduc knocked politely at the front door and then entered with a suit-bag in one hand and a bottle of wine in the other.

Kelly rushed to greet him, positioning herself in such a way that he was forced to hand her the wine bottle and accept the kiss she pressed on his cheek in return. His surprise was evident, but he hid it well before looking up to meet Grey's eyes and return his greeting.

Even the small talk died as Marcel adjourned to the bathroom to shower and change, but Kelly could feel Grey's eyes following her every move as she opened the wine and brought out, significantly, *two* glasses. Then she pretended surprise.

'Oh, I'm so sorry, Mr Scofield. Would you like a glass before you go?' she asked with sickly sweetness and a gleam in his own.

'No, thanks, I'm in a bit of a rush,' he said quietly, hardly bothering to hide what they both knew was a lie. He had been in no hurry at all, and would have enjoyed staying just to dampen the party, but Kelly had to admire his almost arrogant acceptance of her gentle prodding.

'Well, have a nice evening, then,' she smirked. 'Perhaps I'll see you in camp *tomorrow*.'

'Perhaps,' he replied, turning away so quickly she couldn't tell if her gibe had got home or not. Kelly's eyes followed him as he walked to his waiting truck, and she wasn't surprised when he looked back with a casual, frivolous wave.

The rest of the evening, from Kelly's point of view, could only be termed a disaster. It wasn't at all Marcel's fault; the French-Canadian was, if anything, just too gallant and charming for words.

The problem was Kelly herself, and she realised it within five minutes after they arrived at the Golden Star Chinese restaurant in the hired car Marcel had arranged because, in his words, 'one does not take a beautiful woman to dinner in a pick-up truck'.

Kelly had laughed at the formality of such a move, although she did it in such a way that Marcel could only interpret her laughter as a gesture of appreciation for his thoughtfulness. He would have been less pleased, she knew, at her immediate thought that Grey Scofield would never have made such a gesture unless his truck was filthy inside. The grey-eyed camp boss would have automatically presumed that any woman accepting his company would be far more interested in him than his choice of vehicle.

Worse, at least in Kelly's case, he would have been right. Throughout an excellent Chinese dinner in which Marcel kept her exceptionally well entertained, Kelly found herself coping as if she were divided into two people. One Kelly laughed at Marcel's jokes and appreciated his gay flirting and Continental charm; the other wondered where Grey Scofield was dining—and with whom. And wondering, indeed half hoping, that he would be interested enough to check the house later that night to see whether Kelly spent the night alone or not.

Her sleep that night was as fitful as had been her nap in the afternoon. She got to bed before eleven o'clock, after sitting alone for an hour after Marcel dropped her off.

She had been of two minds about his unexpected coolness at the end of the evening, not sure if she was upset or relieved that he had used his long drive as an excuse for the early night and never so much as tried to kiss her goodnight. She had sensed from the beginning that Marcel was an experienced womaniser, but thought she had hidden her own mental divisiveness throughout their dinner date.

But had she? Or had the part of her mind that was preoccupied with thoughts of Grey Scofield communicated her interest in ways that a man of Marcel's experience couldn't miss? She knew that her eyes had subconsciously followed every arrival in the restaurant, that only a part of her mind had been in play while Marcel was plying her with wine and repartee.

And after he had left her with an almost coldly formal adieu, a major part of her consciousness was glad to see the back of him, so that it could concentrate on dealing with this unexpectedly disturbing fixation about Grey Scofield. Grey's name hadn't even been mentioned during the evening, but Kelly knew his presence had been like a ghost at their dinner table, though if Marcel had realised it too he had given no obvious sign.

Only that last-minute coolness, which might have simply been a response to her own. Still, it was mildly disturbing. Bad enough one man who seemed able to read her mind; two would be three too many.

Alone in her bed, she tossed and turned in a fitful attempt at sleep that had her prowling the empty house after midnight, wondering if Grey really did check up on whether Marcel had stayed. And again at two a.m., when some slight noise brought her restlessly and fearfully awake to stalk silently through the darkness, checking doors and windows without finding any reason for her concern.

By four a.m. she had had enough, and after dressing quickly and brewing a Thermos of tea, she slipped through the lightening dawn to start up her truck and head south-ward to Kakwa camp. She could sleep the afternoon away, if necessary, she decided, but even going without sleep would be better than the vague disquiet she felt at the moment.

The drive south was refreshing despite her lack of sleep. She had barely crossed the Wapiti River when a young bull moose shambled out into the roadway ahead of her, dancing along in front of the truck for several hundred metres in that curious rocking gait that looked so ridiculous and yet covered the ground more swiftly than any horse. Kelly laughed at the animal's drooping snout and ungainly trot, thinking that it looked for all the world like a cross between a camel, a mule and a hat-rack.

An old black bear crossed the road ahead of her near the base of Chinook Ridge, rollicking along like a drunken sailor as it spooked upon seeing the truck. She drew abreast of the animal just in time to see the cause of its concern, a cub that was being boosted into a tree just inside the timber.

She was wide awake if slightly lightheaded when she rumbled down the final incline to where the track forked at the Kakwa River, one section veering slightly left towards the old ford, and the other turning hard right to the Kakwa camp itself. The sun was well up despite the early hour, a blessing since the air was still chilly in this altitude, and Kelly stopped her truck and sat for a moment watching the reflection of the sun on the shimmering, tinkling waters of the river. Such clarity, such relatively unspoiled purity, she thought, and for a moment was saddened by the continu-ing development that must eventually have its effect upon the high-country wilderness around her.

She looked downriver, where the crystal waters tumbled across gleaming gravel bars and widened slightly in the approach to the massive waterfall, and then suddenly she seemed to see her dream characters, misty in outline as the sun drew ghostly shapes from the chill of the water.

Kelly shook her head, suddenly frightened that the inexplicable dream should intrude upon her reverie. Damn Grey Scofield anyway, she thought, suddenly adamant in telling herself that he couldn't possibly mean enough to her in any way to create such an effect. She didn't even like the man. He was rough, and crude, and overbearing and dictatorial. Imagine thinking he could dictate her every move!

Looking downriver again, she was suddenly filled with an overwhelming desire to view the famous Kakwa Falls, and even as Grey's warning about going anywhere alone seemed to boom through her mind, she angrily thrust it aside.

It took her only a moment to shift the truck on to the firm tussock-covered bank beside the track, and two minutes later she was walking swiftly down the narrow path beside the river. It was obviously a path beaten down by visitors to the falls, and although originally a game trail it was now so definite that she had little trouble following it.

She wound her way through the tall dark timber, treading carefully over upthrust, exposed roots and chunks of rock in the trail. To her right the river chuckled happily to itself, sometimes out of sight as the trail thrust its way upward to circumnavigate some obstacle, at other times within touching distance as the path wandered right to the riverbank.

It took less than half an hour before Kelly reached the first point at which the falls could be clearly seen, and the view absolutely overwhelmed her. Holding tightly to a mighty tree that clung right to the lip of the canyon, she could look directly down at where the river sprawled lazily against the bedrock before flinging itself down in a shimmering curtain to splash in a large pool far below her.

A huge outcropping in mid-river seemed to divide the waters like a parting in silver hair, allowing two distinct fronds to flow downwards until wind and distance united them again below the outcrop. And beneath it—could it be a cave?

She was too close to get a decent view, so after a moment she returned to the track and began to move even further downstream, now high above the diminutive stream so far below in a narrow, dimly-lit canyon.

The path was less evident now, becoming more of a proper game trail because few visitors wandered so far. To Kelly's inexperienced eye it was difficult to follow, weaving now close to the high rock walls and then inexplicably turning away to thread through the dense timber. After a few minutes she began to worry about her ability to find the way back to the truck, but she carried on, thrusting from her mind the possibility of getting well and truly lost. The river was there, wasn't it? She could hear the thunder of the falls behind her even when they were out of sight. It would be impossible to get lost.

Still, at the first point where she struck what appeared to be a track veering right, closer to the now invisible canyon walls, she took it—and a moment later emerged in a tiny clearing created by the shade of a massive jackpine that perched like a castle on the rim of the canyon. Looking back, she could see the falls clearly for the first time, and the spectacular vista would have taken her breath away if she had had any left.

From nearly half a mile away, the immensity of the falls and the spectacular drop of the deep canyon fell into a perspective impossible to judge from up close, and Kelly understood fully for the first time why local conservationists were so keen to protect this glorious monument to nature. Entranced, she perched for a time on a protruding root of the massive, spreading tree, drinking in the splendour of the view around her.

The utter stillness was so intense, so vivid, that she found herself thinking how true it was that one can sometimes actually *hear* silence. It was almost unnerving.

Below her, shadows danced with the water in the depths of the canyon, while in the falling waters upstream the sunbeams created a rainbow that almost perfectly framed the shallow cave below the falls. The scene was idyllic, and Kelly found herself growing drowsy in the warmth of the sunshine.

Enough of this, she thought. It was high time she was returning to the camp and her duties, or else she would find the abrasive Grey Scofield looking on her absence as the excuse to abuse her in some pointed way. Rising to her feet, Kelly threw one last glance at the beauty of the scene, then began to seek her way back upstream.

It was easier than she had thought; after only a few minutes she reached the fork where she had turned aside to the canyon rim, and shortly afterwards she found herself once again at the lookout directly above the thundering waterfall. Here she paused for another quick look downward, and it was as she straightened up that a flicker of movement in her side-vision brought her erect in wide-eyed horror.

Less than a hundred metres away, fur shining golden and frosty in the sunlight, was an enormous, shambling, humpbacked figure that brought Kelly's heart to her throat. A grizzly bear!

The animal didn't appear to have seen her, but was lazily pawing at some kind of burrow beneath a spreading tree root. Kelly was terror-stricken, almost paralysed with an unreasoning fear. Slowly, step by step and without taking her eyes from the huge creature, she began to back away, feeling for the trail without daring to look for it.

As she retreated, each step seeming an eternity in itself,

her mind whirled with the kaleidoscope of bear stories her father had related to her on his infrequent visits during her childhood. A full-grown grizzly couldn't climb trees. Or could it? She couldn't remember, and it hardly seemed to matter since she, too, would be incapable of climbing a tree in her present state.

And what else? Oh yes, don't run. Any animal will chase something that flees; it's an instinctive reaction. Far different from her own instinctive reaction, which was to turn and run just as fast as she could. Which wouldn't, she knew, be anywhere near fast enough. A grizzly could run down a horse over a short distance, with astounding speed for such a huge beast.

Four steps . . . five . . . six . . . the bear was head-down, peering into the excavation created by its enormous claws . . . seven . . . it was looking directly at her, and Kelly halted like a statue, mesmerised by the tiny, near-sighted eyes that looked at her without seeing. Short-sighted, her father had said, but with nose and ears so keen that vision wasn't terribly important. It would certainly see movement, in any event; Kelly froze.

Eight steps . . . the bear had returned to its digging . . . nine . . . and suddenly it reared upright, looming like a grizzled mountain as it snuffled out its concern in a grunting, pig-like squeal of query.

The bear took a step forward, nose upthrust as it tried to catch her scent. Another, and Kelly felt her breath constricting inside her. She didn't dare to breathe, smothering in her own fear. Another step and she tried to scream.

'Don't move and don't make a sound.' The words hissed in her ear even as a strong hand clasped itself across her mouth, killing the scream before it could escape. An arm wrapped itself around her middle like an iron band, choking away what little air she had inhaled. Kelly would have fainted, but the arm eased immediately and the air rushed in to fill her lungs before fingers of steel closed off her mouth again.

The voice at her ear, even in the hiss of a whisper, was unmistakable. She didn't need to turn and look to know that it was Grey Scofield who held her an immobile captive. And she knew as well that she didn't dare move, not even to look back, because clearly the bear was becoming more agitated.

Its squeal of query had deepened to become a growling demand, and even as she watched, the animal's jaws began to clack together in horrifying fashion, with strings of saliva frothing from the enormous teeth.

'Freeze!' The command was irrelevant; Kelly couldn't have moved had she wanted to. Grey's arms held her actually clear of the ground, and she sensed he was preparing to throw her into the nearest tree if it should become necessary. She could feel the tensing of the muscles as he seemed to flex his arms, like a man preparing to toss the caber in the highland games.

Then, unaccountably, the bear lowered its bulk to four feet again, and with a mighty shake of its head it turned away to fade like pale golden smoke into the foliage. It disappeared so silently, so quickly, that Kelly wondered if it had really been there at all.

The constricting band at her waist eased, only to clamp upon her wrist like a living manacle as Grey thrust Kelly around and began to drag her with him up the trail towards the road.

'Move, dammit!' he growled. 'He'll be circling to catch the wind, and I don't want to be cut off from the trucks.'

So swiftly did he haul her along that Kelly's feet barely touched the rough track beneath them, and when she stumbled it was not to fall, but to be simply hauled through the air like a doll in the hands of a child. Not until they had reached the open space of the road clearing and the comparative safety of the trucks—Grey's parked immediately behind her own—did he allow Kelly to slow to a reasonable pace. And that lasted only a second.

As they reached the truck he suddenly turned her in his hands, forcing her back against the side of the truck as he glared down at her through eyes like pale grey pebbles, blank of all expression in the intensity of his rage.

He seemed to glare at her for hours, but finally his fierce, growling voice invaded the bond of that horrible locking gaze.

'You bloody ... stupid ... little fool!' he grated. 'I should break your silly, childish damned neck for you.'

'I ... I ...' Kelly tried to reply, but her breathlessness and fear made speech impossible. Never had she seen a human being so angry. There was a tangible aura of rage surrounding Grey that was so fearful she would almost sooner have faced the bear.

'You ... nothing!' he snarled. 'Did I or did I not tell you *never* to wander around alone?'

His fingers were like claws digging into her shoulders as he shook her, and Kelly's head snapped forward and back until she thought her neck would snap. She started to try and speak, he didn't give her the chance.

'Damn it! Didn't I?' he demanded, still shaking her.

Tears sprang to her eyes as she tried to speak against the pain of his shaking her, but they did nothing to ease the anger in his eyes. If anything, the expression changed only to one of outright scorn.

'And don't think tears will help you,' he growled. 'You'll be crying a damned sight worse than that before I'm through with you, little miss. My God! If I'd known you were going to be this stupid I'd have packed you out of camp when you first got there.'

Shaking his own head with angry disbelief, he stopped shaking her long enough for her to catch a breath.

'I ... I'm ... I'm sorry,' she managed to say. 'I thought ... thought you meant ... meant ...'

'Think! You didn't think at all and you know it,' Grey snarled. 'What do you think this is, girl, the bloody English countryside? Well, let me tell you, it's not! For somebody who doesn't know what they're up to, it can be a damned dangerous place to be wandering around—especially alone.'

He continued to rail at her, but Kelly no longer heard the individual words. Her head was swimming as the realisation of her earlier danger finally registered. She thought for one horrible moment she was going to be sick.

It seemed like forever until the shaking finally stopped and her vision cleared sufficiently for her to once again face her tormentor. Her long eyelashes fluttered against her tears as she slowly raised her eyes from the deep vee of Grey's half-open shirt front, up the strong column of his neck to the determined chin and the mouth that still quivered with half suppressed anger. And finally to his eyes, deep pools of icy greyness that, just for an instant, seemed to be regarding Kelly with an unexpected tenderness. But even as that thought registered, his eyes glazed over again to become the expressionless, stony orbs that were so much more familiar.

Flexing her shoulders against the harshness of his grasp, Kelly met his gaze squarely despite the fluttering inside her, her own anger beginning to rouse in objection to his angry, rough treatment of her.

Grey regarded her impassively, neither his eyes nor his face giving her any clue to the remaining extent of his anger. But Kelly didn't care. Glaring up at him, she took several deep breaths before she finally spoke.

'Let . . . go . . . of me!' The slowly spaced words emerged in a whisper, but her voice didn't reveal the trembling of white-hot rage inside her. It also had no obvious effect on Grey, who stood unmoving, his hands still firmly gripping her shoulders.

'You . . . swine! You callous, unfeeling swine!' she mouthed, twisting her slim body in a futile attempt to free herself. Still he didn't move.

Thrusting her hands against his massive chest, she

stamped one foot angrily, knowing it was a childish gesture but long past actually caring. It was like shoving against the side of the truck itself; Grey was immobile as a rock. And as silent.

Kelly's plump underlip thrust itself into a determined pout as she glanced down, measuring the position of his legs as she threw back one leg and aimed a vicious kick at his left shin.

This time, adroitly shifting the leg before her toe struck him, Grey laughed, but it was a harsh, cruel laugh that sent shivers up her spine. And then, abruptly, he released her with yet another bark of laughter.

'You've got guts; I'll give you that,' he growled.

Kelly ignored him, turning to fling open the driver's door of her vehicle and begin scrambling up into the high seat. The curse she muttered beneath her breath shouldn't have carried to him, but he heard it. She realised that as one huge hand flashed out to pluck her from the open doorway of the truck and bring her spinning into his arms.

'You ungrateful little vixen,' he whispered harshly before lowering his mouth to claim hers in a harsh, almost brutal kiss that forced apart her lips before she could even think of opposing him.

His arms were wrapped around her middle, crushing the breath from her as his mouth searched her own, demanding, commanding, insisting upon a response.

At first the response was solely negative. Kelly wriggled and kicked and twisted against the grasp that held her helpless, sobbing for breath as his mouth searched across her lips, her cheek, and down against the warm hollow of her shoulder. But resistance was futile, and even before her mind had registered that fact, her body was beginning to betray her with its own response.

She could feel the heat of him, the harsh shifting of his chest muscles against the inflamed softness of her breasts. Her nipples were roused by the pressure, the ceaseless shifting of his denim shirt as it rubbed against them. He was holding her back hard against the side of the truck, his aroused body thrusting against her as he systematically violated her with his mouth.

Kelly's lips softened, her fingers moving of their own volition through the tangled hair on the back of his neck as she shifted her position ever so slightly so as to better meet his passionate lips. She was increasingly conscious of her own arousal, the feel of him pressing her thighs taut and warm despite the thickness of her jeans.

His growling moan of desire was matched then by her own sobbing response as her responses grew freer, more deliberately matched to the contours of his body and the flexing caresses of his hands at her back. His fingers played a throbbing drumroll at the base of her spine, touching off skyrockets of response as they prickled the sensitive nerve endings. Never had she felt such a compelling, demanding response from within herself.

As Grey's lips slid across her cheek to nuzzle beneath the lobe of her ear, Kelly allowed one hand to slacken its grip on his neck, trailing her fingers up along the whiskery line of his jaw, exploring his cheek and forehead before sliding down over the strong lines of his neck to tangle her fingers into the hair of his chest.

As if in response, he slackened his own grip on her, one arm shifting so that his own hand could begin an exploratory journey of its own up her side and across the tautness of her breasts. His every touch like an electric shock, prodding greater and greater responses from her, he used fingers and lips to bring her closer and ever closer to screaming out her demands for surrender.

But it wouldn't really be surrender, she felt. Her body was making demands of its own, thrusting against him, bringing to her lips words of whispered torment and passion as her lips flickered across his ear, guiding his fingers as she twisted herself to make the passage of his hand even more delicious.

Gone was the tiny voice that should have been crying *stop*; Kelly didn't want to stop. She wanted more and more of this man's incredible lovemaking, wanted him to go on holding her, stroking her, fanning the passions she had never before so much as realised could even exist within her.

She was only dimly conscious of Grey freeing one hand long enough to open the door of the truck, then his hands were at her waist, lifting her on to the sun-warmed contours of the seat. She held to him, dragging him in on top of her.

CHAPTER FIVE

THE raucous blare of a truck horn, followed by a chorus of ragged cheers, shattered the idyllic scene with a brutal suddenness.

Grey reared back out of the truck with a bellow of undisguised rage and Kelly thrust herself upright to stare in embarrassed horror at the vehicle which had pulled up squarely beside them. The crowd of laughing, cheering oilmen swam into focus with an alien, inhuman, almost animal aura, and in their faces she didn't see genuine appreciation for the display, but a cruel, mocking derision.

Her head swam, the blood rushing upward to colour her face with the flush of humiliation. How long had they been there? How much had they seen? Then all thoughts of her own embarrassment fled at the sight of Grey rounding the nose of her truck as he advanced like an avenging tiger upon the truckload of laughing men, and for an instant Kelly felt real fear.

But only for an instant; then her unbelieving ears told her that he, too, was laughing, returning ribald jest with one even cruder, more humiliating.

Her eyes grew wide. She honestly did not—could not—believe it. Until a vagrant breeze carried his voice to her, a growling, gravelly voice that mocked her, mocked everything that had gone before as he laughingly taunted the men before him.

She couldn't bear it! Without a conscious thought, she slid over into the driver's seat, started her truck, and slammed it into gear with a vicious yank on the shift lever. The vehicle bucked and coughed at the unaccustomed treatment, and for a single horrifying instant she thought it would stall. But then, thankfully, the co-ordination of clutch and accelerator came together and the truck flung itself off the verge of the track, flinging gravel and dust in a great fan as it slewed on to the track and roared towards Kakwa camp as if all the devils in hell were following.

There was time for only a single glance in the wide rear-view mirrors, but it was enough to show Kelly the agile figure of Grey leaping for his own vehicle, and she had a sudden, almost laughable thought of him thundering in pursuit like the hero of a Western movie. The thought died stillborn in the effort to keep the big truck on the road as she roared down the track at far more speed than was safe.

She arrived in the camp to find the parking lot empty, which was just as well considering the sliding, dust-raising manner in which she flung the truck to a halt before the trailer she now considered home. She didn't bother to take the keys from the truck, much less the various packets she had brought with her from the city. Grabbing the trailer key from the pocket of her jeans, she was out of one door and in through the other before the truck engine could cease coughing.

Inside, the door locked and the security chain fumbled into position, she prowled the interior of the trailer like a demented soul. Gone were the tears, replaced by confusion.

How could Grey have made love to her like that, and then walked over to those other men and *laughed* about it? And how could she have let him . . . helped him . . . make love to her in such a totally wanton fashion?

Even in the throes of her despair, Kelly couldn't ignore or excuse her own part in the prelude to that provident but humiliating interruption. She had responded to Grey with an abandon that in retrospect frightened her far more than did the bear. And he had laughed!

Shame gave way to rage, bitter rage that coursed through her slender young body as quickly as passion had coursed only minutes earlier. The nerve of Grey Scofield!

Kelly stalked through the trailer, her anger growing with the certain knowledge that within minutes he would be pounding on the door, demanding entrance.

For what? To apologise . . . it was too late for that. To explain his chauvinistic, mocking attitude . . . what possibly could be explained? He had cut her to the very soul, and even an overbearing, arrogant animal like him should realise that.

Sensitive ears, awareness heightened by her anger, picked up the sound of Grey's truck arriving. Kelly flung herself down in a chair, rose, sat in another chair, then scurried into the bathroom. She could not face him, had no intention of doing so, yet her ears strained for the sound of him coming to her door.

And strained in vain. After minutes of torture and anticipation she had to accept it. He wasn't even going to try and apologise!

Kelly fussed and fumed, staring into the bathroom mirror at a face pale with emotion, the freckles standing out in stark relief. Her eyes were puffy, not from crying but from holding back the tears, and even as she stared at a strangely unfamiliar countenance in the mirror, her head began to throb.

The throbbing intensified with the growl of truck engines as an entire flotilla of vehicles swarmed into the compound, forming a line in front of the dining trailer. Rushing to the door of her own trailer, Kelly was mystified for only as long as it took her to look at the clock. It read seven-fifteen, and she realised with a start that it was just breakfast time; obviously the men had been out working, taking full advantage of the long northern daylight when the sun stretched out of bed as early as four a.m.

And with the realisation came her own hunger, a sudden ravishing hunger spurred by the raging passions within her. She reached for the doorknob, then paused. Could she bring herself to enter the dining hall, to face Grey Scofield and perhaps the jeering of a room full of men? She had a visualisation of Grey holding forth at great length, entertaining his crew with a bawdy tale of his own before-breakfast exploits. At *her* expense.

'Well, damn Grey Scofield!' she muttered, flinging open the door and marching determinedly towards the mess hall. The hazy yet all too vivid memories of the truck-load of jeering men revealed no familiar faces, and in her present mood Kelly didn't really care. Let him tell the whole camp, if he liked; she didn't care.

There was no jeering when Kelly entered the mess trailer, only the expectable chorus of greetings from men intent on stuffing themselves with enormous quantities of bacon and eggs, steak and hash-brown potatoes, stacks of hot buttered toast and pots of steaming, strong black coffee. Grey Scofield, she noted with some surprise, wasn't there.

Kelly ducked through the serving hatch and checked quickly that she wasn't needed, then loaded a plate of her own and wandered over to sit at an empty table, her back to the thinning crowd of men. She didn't want conversation, didn't especially want the gentle teasing flirtatiousness of some of the younger men in the camp. She wanted to be alone with her thoughts of anger and humiliation and revenge.

'When you're finished you'd best go apologise to your truck.'

The words thrust rudely into her thoughts, words in a voice like shifting gravel, and Kelly looked up to meet Grey's eyes as he slid into a seat across from her, depositing a well-laden breakfast tray down in front of him.

'Do you mind?' she replied haughtily, the rejection in her voice as cold as her eyes.

'No, but the truck probably does,' he replied calmly. 'You should know better than to treat an innocent vehicle like that.'

'I really don't know what you're talking about,' she

answered, hiding the lie behind a quick mouthful of toast.

'Like hell you don't! Personally I couldn't care less if you're angry with me, but I wish you wouldn't take it out on the machinery,' he replied.

'Frankly I don't see that it's any of your business,' Kelly said, lowering her eyes from the piercing gaze of his own.

'Everything that happens in this camp is my business,' he said. 'And while I suppose I can't blame you for being angry, it hurts a little to see you being stupid.'

'Oh, isn't that just *too* bad,' she simpered. 'And here I thought you might have been worried about me having an accident or something. But it wasn't that, of course. You were just worried about the poor truck.'

'Exactly,' he snapped, eyes suddenly chillingly cold. 'If I worried about every weird thing you do, my girl, I'd give myself ulcers before the end of the summer.'

'Well, when I get back into the kitchen you might end up with worse than that,' she snarled in return. 'I'd try wolf poison, but I doubt if it works on animals of the lower type—like rats.'

'Threats again? I really thought you'd have learned your lesson last time,' replied Grey. Then he smiled horribly at the look on her face. They both remembered the fiasco of the first revenge attempt, but only she could remember it as a horrible defeat.

'My God, but you're a smug, superior sort of creature!' she retorted.

'Superior, definitely. But seldom smug,' he grinned.

'Well then, stop laughing at me; just finish your breakfast and go off and do whatever it is you do,' she snapped. 'I really *had* hoped to enjoy my breakfast in peace.'

His soft reply was lost in the sudden shuffling sound as the remaining men stacked their breakfast trays and fled the mess trailer in a body. Kelly realised that they were only anxious to get back to their work, but it seemed as if they had obeyed some unspoken command from their leader, and she rebelled at the thought.

'There,' he said quietly. 'Now everybody's gone, we're alone here, so go ahead and throw something at me or whatever and get some of the poison out of your system. Go ahead! It'll do you good.'

Kelly's anger flared at his insolence, fanned by the fact that she had been thinking of doing exactly what he had advised. He was totally insufferable!

'I think you're fantasising just a little,' she replied with a calmness she didn't feel. 'There's certainly no poison in *my* system, and I can't imagine you being significant enough to bother throwing anything at.'

To her surprise, he laughed aloud. 'I always reckoned I was a lover, not a fighter,' he chuckled. 'Nice to see I'm not the only one.'

'Well, personally I'd rather fight,' she retorted. 'Even if you're not much good at it, it couldn't be much worse than your lovemaking.'

'Funny,' he replied, 'but I'd be more likely to put it the other way around. Sure as hell your loving is better than your fighting; that much I'm certain of.'

'Don't overrate yourself,' Kelly replied. 'You really haven't enough experience with either one to be making such a sweeping judgment.'

'Ah, but I have—and what's more I've got witnesses to prove it,' he grinned, and Kelly winced at the realisation that he had deliberately led her into that reply, like a fish to the bait.

'Well, I just hope they don't believe everything they see,' she replied blindly, already struggling to her feet in the hope that she could flee before the tears came.

'So do I,' he replied, and the sudden calm seriousness in his voice made her glance up just as his hands closed upon her shoulders, drawing her against him. 'I'd hate for them . . . for anybody . . . to think it was as casual a thing as it looked.'

The strength of him seemed to flow to her through his hands, a strength that mingled with the still-smouldering anger inside her. Kelly stamped her small foot as she wriggled free of his grasp and stepped back to glare angrily up at him.

'Well, I'd hate for them to think it was anything *but* casual!' she snapped. And ignoring the angry pain in his eyes, she turned and dashed through the doorway, fleeing blindly until she had reached the sanctuary of her trailer.

Damn the man! He couldn't be doing anything but toying with her, unaware of how much he affected her, she thought. Or else all too aware of it, which was even worse. But she watched with unexpectedly mixed feelings as he stomped angrily to his truck and drove out of the camp.

Kelly was much less hostile when she finally woke after a three-hour afternoon nap, but whatever she might have said to Grey was left unsaid, because he didn't show up for dinner that night, nor for breakfast the next day. Stranger, none of the men engaged in their usual speculation about his whereabouts, so that when he still didn't return the following night Kelly was none the wiser.

She herself had been busy enough with administrative work that she only consciously missed his presence at meal-times, and in the quiet hours of the fading mountain twilight when even the birds seemed to be silenced by the clear, still air and the incredible smells of high-country plants.

She was busy once again with paperwork the following morning, revelling in the quiet of an empty camp, when the throbbing vibration of an approaching helicopter brought her out of the office trailer to stand in wonder as it settled like some gigantic dragonfly in the centre of the parking lot.

The wonder increased as the door opened to reveal a pair of stunning, nylon-clad legs that were quickly followed by a shapely, modern-dressed body and a thatch of expertly cut blonde hair. Kelly was suddenly over-conscious of her crude pony-tail and stained jump-suit, not to mention her total lack of make-up, but she put on a smile of welcome as the blonde approached her.

'Good morning,' she said pleasantly, expecting to receive at least a smile in return. But the blonde only looked through her as if she didn't exist.

The pale, cold eyes flickered over her, dismissed her as insignificant, then roamed across the empty camp with a faintly predatory look before returning to meet Kelly's gaze.

'Mr Scofield . . . where is he?' The words emerged in a sibilant hiss, tinged with an accent that Kelly could recognise only as Scandinavian.

'He isn't here, I'm afraid,' she replied calmly.

'I can see that,' retorted the blonde. 'I asked where he is.'

'I really don't know,' Kelly replied with a coldness of her own. And I really don't care, she thought silently. But you do, don't you?

'He will be returning for luncheon?' It was more statement than question, leaving Kelly fumbling slightly for a reply.

'I . . . I really don't know,' she said, suddenly angry at her own reticence. 'Would you like to come and have coffee . . . or something while you wait for him?'

'No!' The word was thrust out aggressively. 'I do not wait for him. You will tell him that Freda was here.' The blonde was half turned away when Kelly spoke out.

'Freda . . .?'

The blonde turned back with a silky grin, the smarmy grin of a woman who could view a girl like Kelly as totally insignificant. 'Freda Jorgensen,' she replied in a tone that implied it was a name to be recognised and reckoned with. 'But he will know.'

And she was gone, sliding lithely into the open bubble of the helicopter and slamming the door as it began to thrust its way back into the sparkling blue of the mountain sky.

'Wowee! Wasn't that something else?' came a sign of vivid appreciation from behind Kelly, and she turned to see Fred Griffiths looking longingly after the departing helicopter.

'Yes, it was, rather,' Kelly agreed, then smiled at his look of adoration. She enjoyed bantering with Fred, whose quiet manner hid a sharp, rapier wit that was far closer to the British sense of humour than that of most men she had met in Canada.

'Too bad she wouldn't stay for coffee,' he said sadly, turning away to resume his work in the kitchen. 'Sure would be a change from this scruffy bunch of yahoos we're cooking for now.' Then he looked at Kelly with sudden realisation. 'Oh, I didn't mean you, of course. It's just that . . .'

'It's just that blondes have more fun,' she replied bitterly. 'I understand, Fred.' And then, much more lightly, 'Maybe if you're a good boy, somebody'll buy you one for Christmas.'

'Humph! I couldn't afford to feed it,' he replied, turning back to the kitchen with a broad grin.

Grey Scofield could afford to feed it, Kelly mused as she returned to her own work after leaving a note on his desk to inform him of his visitor.

Surprisingly enough, she then forgot about the visitor until a knock at her door that evening brought her face to face with Grey, who held the note in his hand as he stood at the step leading into the trailer.

'Doesn't say much, this note,' he said quietly.

'Neither did Miss Jorgensen,' Kelly replied tautly, her entire body suddenly tense just at the sight of him.

Grey flashed her a sardonic grin. 'You don't sound like you were much impressed,' he said.

'Not especially,' she blurted, and then, 'although she's certainly very beautiful.'

'And rich. You might as well add that in as well.'

'I didn't know it.'

'No, you wouldn't, I suppose. Her father is Sven Jorgensen, who would be one of the biggest private oil magnates in Canada,' he said. 'I do a fair bit of work for him.'

'I see. Well, that explains why she has a private helicopter to do her visiting in,' Kelly replied, shuddering inside at such a singularly bitchy remark.

If Grey noticed it, he didn't show the awareness in his cool grey eyes. 'I suppose you thought at first she was in one of my helicopters,' he replied with a mocking grin.

'Since I didn't know you owned any, the thought didn't occur to me,' Kelly replied. 'Besides, the one she was in had the company name written all over it. Even I couldn't miss that.'

'Well, I'm glad there's something you don't miss,' he replied in a cold, flat voice. 'What I'd like to know now is what happened to the papers she said she'd leave with you. I expected to find them in the office when I got here, and all I found was this rather terse little note.'

Kelly reeled with the shock of it. That bitch! she thought. It became amazingly obvious just how she had been set up, but she couldn't believe such a thing could happen. There was no reason for Freda Jorgensen to do such a thing, but it had obviously been done.

'I'm afraid I don't understand,' she said. 'Miss . . . Jorgensen brought nothing with her, gave nothing to me. She only said to tell you she'd been here, that's all.'

'Oh, come now, Kelly. She flew all the way out here specifically to bring me the bloody documents. And you expect me to sit here and believe she just turned around and flew away again without leaving them?' Grey's tone was mockingly incredulous.

'Personally I don't care *what* you think,' Kelly snarled. 'She came, she said to tell you she was here, and she left again. Full stop. She had no documents with her that I saw, she never mentioned any documents to me—and I must say, Mr Scofield, that I damned well don't like the insinuations you're making!'

'I'm not making any insinuations,' he growled in return. 'It was agreed that Freda would leave the documents with you if I wasn't here. If you say she didn't, okay. I'm not calling you a liar and I'm not accusing you of anything, so stop going all prissy about it. I just want to know what happened to my documents, that's all.'

'Well then, I suggest you ask the person who had them last,' retorted Kelly. 'Which, if I may remind you, wasn't me. Now if that's all you've come to talk about I'd like to get to bed; I'm rather tired.'

'Right. Goodnight, then,' he said, turning away abruptly to walk swiftly back towards his own quarters and leaving Kelly standing dumbly on her doorstep, her lips framed silently around her own goodnight.

Kelly slept badly, her mind troubled by the deliberate attempt by Freda Jorgensen to put her into a bad light. There seemed, on the surface of it, no logical explanation, she thought. She had never before met the woman, and she was relatively certain the blonde wouldn't have noticed her on those occasions she had seen Freda in restaurants.

Could Grey have mentioned Kelly to Freda? It also seemed rather unlikely, and yet the blonde woman had quite deliberately engineered her visit so as to see Kelly, and apparently to cause trouble for her as well.

Why? She gnawed at the problem throughout the early hours of the night, and as a result finally got to sleep so late that she overslept in the morning. It was only the sound of an approaching helicopter that startled her into wakefulness.

Peering from her trailer window, she saw immediately that Freda Jorgensen had returned, and when the woman stepped down from helicopter bubble she clearly held a sheaf of documents in one manicured hand. That was all

Kelly noticed; she herself raced to the bathroom and did her quickest-ever job of washing away the sleep from her eyes and preparing to meet the world.

For world, read Freda-bitch-Jorgensen, Kelly mused, brushing rapidly at her long red hair and idly wishing it was slightly shorter and more manageable.

Make-up? No, she thought. She was out of the habit, and to arrive wearing it would be simply too obvious. There was no way she could openly compete with Freda's blonde loveliness anyway.

It wasn't until she had slipped into a clean blouse and jeans and was reaching for her sandals that the enormity of her thinking suddenly came clear to her. Competing? Competing for the attentions of a man she had almost surrendered to only days before, yet spurned haughtily only last night? A man she was quite prepared to dislike intensely?

'I must be going mad,' she said absently to her image in the bathroom mirror. It was one thing to face the fact that Grey Scofield desired her, or indeed that she felt a strong physical attraction for him. But the strength of that attraction was quite something else again, and when she emerged from her trailer for the short but seemingly endless walk to the kitchen complex, there was a new, almost alien seriousness in her manner.

Her mood was not improved by the absence of both Grey and Freda. Kelly had a frightening mental picture of them sharing a tall, cool drink—and what else?—in Grey's quarters, then shook the image aside as she buried herself in the task of checking out the quantities in the larder.

But her senses were tuned to Grey, a fact she was forced to realise when the dining room door opened and she knew without looking that it was he who had entered. The staccato click of high heels following him in was all the confirmation Kelly required, so she wasn't surprised when she heard him ask Marie about getting some coffee.

Kelly came within an inch of shouting that coffee wasn't available outside meal hours, then derided herself for ever thinking in so petty a fashion.

When the coffee was ready, she said, 'I'll take it out, Marie,' and promptly did so. Grey looked up with vague surprise when Kelly deposited the tray on the table between himself and Freda, but his expression quickly cleared when she merely nodded and turned to leave without speaking.

'Hang on a minute, Kelly,' he said. 'You haven't actually met Freda, have you?' Surprised, Kelly could only shake her head and stand while he formulated a brief introduction.

It was no consolation to be met by a dazzling smile from the tall Scandinavian, who immediately launched into an apology for the mix-up over the documents.

'It was my fault entirely and I still don't know how it happened,' she explained in her husky, lilting voice. 'But when I found out that Grey wasn't here as expected, I forgot all about the documents until he radioed last night. Papa was not amused, as they say, and I understand Grey was perfectly beastly to you about it.'

'Hardly beastly,' Kelly replied with a shrug, unable to match the woman's buoyant approach with the haughty snub of the day before.

'Oh, but he's always beastly, aren't you, darling?' Freda replied, reaching out to stroke Grey's bare forearm with her long, perfectly-manicured nails. 'Now you must apologise to Kelly, and she must forgive you and join us for coffee. Please, I insist,' she snapped, as Kelly made to turn away.

'Really it isn't necessary,' said Kelly, who wanted only to get away from the pair of them. She was intensely conscious of Grey's eyes upon her, savouring her discomfort, and beneath the bantering of Freda's manner she sensed the seriousness of a cat watching a mouse.

Freda Jorgensen combined beauty and sophistication with a thinly-disguised feline instinct that Kelly knew she couldn't possibly combat. Kelly was, normally, a direct and open person, she lacked the predatory instincts that glowed from the blonde beauty like an aura.

'I do apologise, Kelly,' came the growling, gravelly voice of the man who so thoroughly sparked Freda's cattiness, and the voice played upon Kelly's heart-strings like the fingers of a concert musician. Her legs turned to water and she felt a strange warmth floating into her middle.

'I said it wasn't necessary,' she replied with unexpected calmness. 'You have the documents, and that's certainly all that's important. Now if you'll excuse me, I have a great deal of work to do.' She turned and fled before Grey could speak again, hating herself for her cowardice but unable to handle the sudden realisation that she was far too nearly in love with Grey for her own good.

'Stupid, stupid, stupid,' she chanted to herself as she blindly tried to itemise the contents of the huge pantry a few moments later. The violent jealousy that had surged up in her when Freda had touched Grey's arm frightened her even more in retrospect than it had at the time.

Hiding in her work, Kelly was nonetheless totally aware when Freda's helicopter throbbed into the sky about an hour later, and when the men began noisily filing into the dining room for lunch, she took great care to keep to her work behind the scenes. Seeking seclusion became more difficult after lunch, when even Kelly had to admit there was nothing left for her to do in the kitchen.

Her two cooks were both surprised and delighted, albeit slightly suspicious, when she shooed them off for an afternoon's fishing and took over the preparation of that night's dinner herself, working with a single-minded intensity that brought strange, curious looks but no comments from Marie.

Grey made an appearance at dinner, but apart from a

mildly curious glance kitchenward when he saw the meal being offered, he showed no sign of awareness about Kelly's work.

The cooks returned just before dark, weary after a long climb to the river below the falls and the seemingly longer climb up again under the burden of several very large Dolly Varden char. They received Kelly's congratulations with somewhat guilty reserve, still unsure what had sparked their unexpected holiday, but brightened visibly when she offered to cook the fish for them in a special breakfast production.

She was up at four, bustling about the silent kitchen as she prepared a special sauce and basting mixture for the fish, and had everything ready so the cooks could have their meal and still be on duty before the main camp breakfast.

She had just admitted her fishermen to the dining hall, cautioning them to quiet so as to avoid waking the rest of the camp, when a light tap on the kitchen door brought her guiltily to her feet. It was no surprise to find Grey looking at her through the screen, one eyebrow raised in sardonic amusement as he surveyed the beautifully displayed fish, one baked and the other poached to a perfect texture in a creamy sauce.

'So this is how you keep your cooks so happy,' he growled, 'little special treats and afternoons off to go fishing.'

'I don't see that it's any business of yours,' Kelly replied abruptly, mildly put out by his innuendo.

'Obviously. Nobody invited me to share the feast,' he replied with a grin, knowing that his authority would force an invitation from one or the other of the cooks.

'There's room for one more, but only if the chef doesn't mind,' Fred Griffiths replied softly, his patient, gentle eyes revealing his dislike at being trapped in such a position.

'And do you mind?' Grey asked quietly. 'I'd just like to try a bit, not do you out of *your* share or anything.'

Kelly most assuredly did mind, but she also knew she didn't dare reveal it too strongly. It was bad enough having Grey catch them at their feast, without bothering to go into vivid explanations about why they should appear to be being sneaky about it.

Grey caught her hesitation. 'I understand that you're not allowed to serve wild game or fish as part of your catering to the camp,' he said calmly. 'Which includes me, technically, but I won't tell if you don't.'

He understood only too well. It was perfectly all right for Kelly to serve the fishermen their own catch, but any hint that wild game was being included in the general catering at the camp would mean the end of her father's business at worst and a heavy fine at best. Kelly would have had no compunction about using such an excuse if Grey himself hadn't raised it; now sheer good manners prohibited such a move and they both knew it.

'Since you were invited, I can't imagine that being a problem,' she said with carefully rehearsed graciousness. 'Just sit down, then, and I'll fetch another plate.'

His appreciation of her culinary efforts surpassed even that of her two cooks, whose approval was based on technical merits and was, Kelly knew, well enough deserved. Even she herself was rather impressed with the fish, which was a variety she had neither cooked nor tasted before.

'Ah, you'll make somebody a wonderful wife some day,' Grey sighed, lighting a cigarette and leaning back into his chair after the meal was done. His remark was a cliché, and the worse for being deliberate, but Kelly couldn't help rising to the bait.

'There's far more to being a wife than just good cooking, I should imagine,' she replied in tones that implied a distinct lack of interest in the topic.

'And sarcasm isn't part of it,' he replied brightly. 'No man should be expected to thrive on a diet of hot tongue and cold shoulder.'

The retort drew a chuckle of appreciation from the two

cooks, who were silenced just as quickly by a glare from Kelly. Then, realising how silly she must look, she countered with a line of her own. 'A diet that's too bland will only make you fat and complacent,' she retorted, unsmiling eyes directing the remark squarely at Grey.

'Fat, maybe. Complacent, never,' he replied laughingly. 'I couldn't stand to live with a woman who made me complacent.'

Too true, Kelly thought. Living with Grey Scofield would be likely to include just about anything—except boredom. Living with Grey Scofield . . . For just an instant she shivered deliciously at the thought, but then she met his laughing, mocking eyes and retreated.

Fred Griffiths wisely interrupted with a comment that changed the line of the conversation, and the talk stayed on safe ground then until the arrival of Marie Cardinal warned them it was time to start preparing breakfast for the camp. Kelly instinctively headed back to her supply room, but was halted by Grey's hand on her shoulder.

'Can you spare me a minute in your office?' he said. 'There are things I'd like to discuss before I head into town this morning.'

Kelly wanted to refuse, knowing she really didn't want to be alone with Grey under any conditions, but she couldn't very well say so with other people around, so she merely nodded. When his fingers left her shoulder to hold open the door for her, she could still feel the tingle of their touch as she walked across the gravelled compound towards her own trailer.

Once inside, Grey flung himself idly into the depths of a convenient armchair, but Kelly perched herself alertly on a stool behind the counter, feeling vaguely more secure with the structure between them. He sat quietly observing her as he lit up a cigarette, then finally spoke.

'First off, I honestly do want to apologise about that misunderstanding over the documents,' he said.

'There's nothing to apologise for,' Kelly retorted almost angrily. 'Actually I thought you must have forgotten about it; I certainly did,'

Grey nodded, not bothering to hide the growing amusement in his eyes. 'Okay,' he said finally. 'We'll consider it forgotten along with your rather rude treatment of Freda Jorgensen.' Kelly bristled at the mention of the name, then quickly calmed herself. She had been rude, perhaps, but nothing like the rudeness Freda had shown during their first meeting. But then Grey knew nothing about that, and nothing she could say would ever explain the innate hostility that existed between her and Freda.

'No comment?' Grey didn't look overly surprised, and Kelly immediately thought he was baiting her.

'No . . . should there be?' she replied. 'I thought it was all . . . forgotten . . . not brought up for comment.'

Grey shook his head. 'Okay, you win. But you were rude, and you damned well know it, too. Frankly I couldn't care less, except that it's so out of character for you it bothers me just a little.'

'Well, I certainly shouldn't let it if I were you,' Kelly replied tartly. 'Especially considering that you know absolutely nothing about my character in the first place.'

'Hah! I wouldn't go so far as to say that,' he replied with a knowing grin. 'I probably know far more about your character than you imagine. I surely know how you react to certain . . . physical . . . stimuli.'

'Which has nothing whatsoever to do with character, as someone like you should know all too well,' she retorted. 'And now if you're finished chastising me, I have quite a lot of work to . . .'

'Ah, come off it,' he interrupted. 'We both know you've got this place so organised it could run without you lifting a finger, so stop kidding around. You don't want to be alone with me, and that's all there is to it.'

'Whatever you say, Mr Scofield, sir,' Kelly replied. 'I

have far better things to do than argue with you.'

'I doubt that too,' he said, grinning mischievously. 'Unless of course you count early morning treats for the cooks. Almost enough to make me wish I'd taken up cooking myself.'

'Since it isn't something I intend to make a habit of, I expect you'd be wasting your time,' Kelly replied. 'Besides, I'm rather choosy about whom I select for what you call treats.'

'And so you should be. Which brings me to my second point of this little discussion,' Grey replied. 'This top cook of yours—Griffiths—how good is he?'

'Fred? Why, he's . . . he's very good indeed,' she said. 'Your own stomach should tell you that.' And then, very tartly, 'But then of course you're so seldom here to eat that maybe you hadn't . . .'

'Enough, enough! I know he's a good cook, but that wasn't really what I meant. How is he on the admin side? Like, could he take over here for, say, a week on his own?'

'I don't see why not, provided there was somebody to make the supply runs for him,' Kelly answered. 'I shouldn't want to expect him to take quite the responsibility I do for no financial reward.'

'Good!' Grey looked down at his cigarette and took a thoughtful pull at it. 'Want to spend a week in Calgary?'

'I'm afraid I don't understand.' Kelly understood only too well what he seemed to be implying, but she didn't dare risk a blatant accusation. It would be too like Grey Scofield to have just the answer to make her look totally ridiculous.

'I want you to come to Calgary with me for a week, that's all,' he said, eyes twinkling in barely-suppressed amusement as he correctly read her consternation.

'I'm afraid I couldn't do that,' she finally replied after an uncomfortably long hesitation.

'Why not?'

'Well, for one thing your offer doesn't especially interest

me,' she said, choking back a growing anger at his suave, mocking attitude. 'And for another I don't feel that I warrant such a holiday. After all, I am responsible for the catering here, or had you forgotten that?'

'How could I possibly forget?' Grey smiled. Then he was silent for some time, his eyes drinking in Kelly's swiftly diminishing serenity.

'So you don't want to come?'

'I don't think I should, no.'

'That isn't what I asked. Do you want to come or not?'

'Not!' She forced determination into her voice.

'Okay.' Grey shrugged as if it no longer mattered to him. 'What do you want me to tell your father?'

'What has he got to do with this?' Kelly could feel the beginnings of an awful suspicion.

'Well, I've got to give him some reason for you not coming with us. Although I suppose he'll settle for the fact that you just don't like my company.'

'It would be no more than the truth,' Kelly replied with growing anger. 'And that's considerably more than you're giving me. Why, may I ask, would you be thinking of taking my father to Calgary, of all places?'

'Well he's sure as hell not coming down here when they let him out of hospital,' Grey replied. 'And I don't like the idea of leaving him alone in Grande Prairie; he'd only be trying to get back to work before he should.'

'Surely not!'

Grey looked at her with undisguised amusement. 'You really don't know your old dad all that well, do you? If it wasn't for a deal I made with some of the nurses there, he'd already be trying to get back to work from his hospital bed. Here he'd be impossible.'

'At least here I should be able to care for him,' Kelly said sternly.

'He'd walk all over you and be back running the show within a week,' said Grey. 'You'd have no more chance of keeping him properly subdued and resting than fly to the moon.'

'And just who is supposed to "subdue" him in Calgary, may I ask?' she responded.

'My own dear old mother, that's who,' he replied with a grin. 'And don't knock it, dearie. My old mom could keep your dad, you, and me in line without even breathing hard.'

'You're ... you're taking him to your home, then?' Kelly was becoming increasingly confused by Grey's attitude and his apparent refusal to give her any more details than he thought she needed to know.

'That's right. He and Mom are old friends, and she's got nothing much else to do anyway. She'd love to have him and it'll make things easier all around. I've got enough troubles worrying about you, without having your dad on my mind too.'

He was teasing her, and she knew it, but she couldn't hold her tongue. 'You have absolutely no business worrying about me, *Mr* Scofield,' she said scathingly, 'and I'm more than capable of looking after my father and administering the affairs of his business as required.'

'That's your story, you stick to it,' he growled, 'but your dad's going to Calgary whether you like it or not. What I want to know is whether you're coming for a week or so just to see him properly settled in.'

'Of course I am,' she cried angrily.

'Good. I knew you'd change your mind.' He grinned at her engagingly. 'Sure took you long enough, though.'

'What! You ... you deliberately misled me about the whole thing,' Kelly retorted. 'You deliberately made me think ... oh, never mind.'

'Oh no, you don't get off that easily. What did I *deliberately* make you think? That I wanted you to spend a week with me in Calgary? What's wrong with that? Or did you put something into the invitation, little Miss Priss?

Like maybe I'm after your fair virgin body? Is that it?
Come on, admit it.'

Kelly couldn't quite meet his eyes, mostly because he
was so aggressively right, but also because in retrospect she
realised that she had found the idea far more attractive
than she must ever let him realise.

'When shall we be going to pick up my father?' she asked
in a deliberate change of subject.

'I don't know yet. Probably tomorrow or the next day.
That's if I decide to let you come along. You did refuse,
after all.'

This time she had to meet his eyes, but the mockery she
was expecting didn't make itself obvious. Instead there was
a chilling seriousness in Grey's eyes that Kelly found distinctly unnerving. 'But . . . but you have to take me. You
just have to,' she stammered.

'Have to? Let's get something straight, little red fox. I
don't *have to* do anything of the sort. Matter of fact, maybe
I should just forget about the whole thing. It might teach
you not to take people for granted so quickly.'

'But I . . . I . . .'

'But you *nothing*! You know damned well you thought I
was trying to organise some kind of seduction attempt, and
I should point out that I'm rather capable of less clumsy
approaches than that. You thought a lot of things, but you
haven't yet thought that maybe an apology is in order.'

'An apology? Why, you . . .'

'Now, now, temper! You don't want to upset me, remember. Because if you do I might get really firm about
not taking you. As it stands, you can still convince me, if
you want to go badly enough.'

Kelly battened down her temper. Everything inside her
was screaming angrily at the audacity of this tall, hard-
eyed man, but he held the whiphand and they both knew
it. 'What . . . what must I do to convince you?' she asked in
a meek, barely audible voice.

She was looking down at the floor, afraid to meet his eyes lest he see the mixture of rage and confusion in her own, so his lithe movement in rising surprised her. One instant he was lounging relaxed in the chair; the next he was standing tall in front of her, one hand reaching to lift her chin.

'Well, a kiss would be a nice *start*,' he drawled quietly. And before she could answer, his lips descended upon her own with a solid mastery that obliviated any possible reply.

As his lips met hers, Kelly felt him drop his hand from her chin, removing any restraint upon her. But she didn't move, just stood there and let his lips move strong and searchingly over her mouth. He would think she wasn't responding, she thought, but he could never know that her stillness was not to keep from betraying displeasure, but to keep from revealing how much she wanted his arms to close around her, his mouth to begin a pattern of ravishment into which she could enter wholeheartedly.

The kiss went on and on and on, and although only their mouths touched, Kelly could feel the sexual tension as it flowed like electricity between them. Her body was rigid, hands clenched into tiny fists at her sides as she resisted the desire to fling them around Grey's neck. He began to raise his head and she couldn't help but raise herself on tiptoe, clinging to his lips as if held by a magnet.

Until he lifted his head too far, and she felt his lips release her even as they twisted into the slightest of mocking sneers. 'Yes,' he said, 'a rather nice beginning indeed. Now where do we go from here, I wonder . . . into the fair maiden's trundle bed, perhaps?'

His attitude, and the look in his fierce eyes, told her he wasn't jesting. Worse, he had no look of loving, even liking in his eyes. He wanted her, desired her, but nothing beyond that. And he would have her if he pleased . . . whether she wanted it or not. Kelly shook her head in approaching panic.

'No . . . no, please,' she whispered.

She wanted Grey, wanted him in every possible way that any woman could want a man. But not like this, not with no semblance of mental rapport, not as a form of emotional and physical blackmail.

And yet, she knew, if he were to take her in his arms and carry her to the bed . . . with even a hint of love . . .

'Hm!' he grunted. 'Ah well, I suppose I shouldn't have expected you to be suitably co-operative.' And then, to her horror, he did exactly what she had been thinking of. Strong hands clasped themselves about her upper arms as he turned her before lifting her into his arms as he strode towards the looming shape of the double bed.

'No!' Kelly cried. 'Oh, no!' She began to twist and squirm in his arms, reaching up to claw at his hair as her eyes grew wide with real terror. She just couldn't let him take her like this, no matter what the incentive, no matter what the power he could hold over her.

She landed on the bed with a thud that shook the entire trailer, still writhing and fighting for the seconds it took her to realise that Grey wasn't on the bed with her, but was standing over her with a wry grin on his face. Only the grin didn't extend into his eyes, which held an undeniable passion.

There was a trace of pink alongside one eye where her nails had caught him, but otherwise he was unmarked by the assault except for the harshness of his breathing. His eyes burned down at her like beams of frozen light, but he said nothing as they raked across the curves of her body. And then, abruptly, he turned on his heel and strode quickly from the trailer, slamming the door so hard that the entire structure rocked on its springs.

CHAPTER SIX

TEN minutes later Kelly watched through tear-reddened eyes as the tall figure of Grey Scofield slid into the driver's seat of his personal pick-up truck, which then lumbered slowly towards the compound entrance. She wasn't surprised that Grey made no attempt to so much as glance towards her trailer, and couldn't help wondering if he would ever bother to tell her when he got news of her father's release from hospital.

She was still standing by the window when a blaring horn signalled the arrival of a new vehicle, which sped into the parking lot and slid to a halt before Kelly's trailer. Marcel Leduc, looking even more slender than usual in a pair of tight-fitting blue jeans and a shirt half open to his narrow waist, slid from the driver's seat and strode impatiently to meet Kelly at the trailer door.

'*Mon Dieu!* You look as angry as that Scofield person, who almost ran me off the road back there,' he exclaimed. 'And I suppose it has been him that makes you cry.'

Marcel didn't wait for an answer, probably didn't even want one. 'And so it is perhaps a good thing that I have arrived with such good news,' he said. 'It is not good for someone so beautiful to be all red-eyed and weepy.'

'I could use some good news,' Kelly admitted, smiling in spite of her mood at Marcel's intriguing use of his second language.

'*Bien!* Just so long as you don't snap off my head, like Scofield has done when I tell him about it,' Marcel replied. 'One would think he would be pleased to hear that your father will be coming from the hospital tomorrow, but no! I tell him and he merely snarls at me as if I am the bringer of bad news instead of good.'

'Tomorrow? Oh, thank goodness!' Kelly cried, her mind already leaping ahead to begin planning for the big event. But she sobered quickly with the realisation that her father's release meant yet another confrontation with Grey.

Marcel was quick to spot her change of mood, and under his rapid-fire questioning Kelly had little choice but to reveal Grey's plans for both her and her father. But if she expected support from the French-Canadian, she was mistaken.

'Scofield is right, of course,' Marcel said immediately. 'Your father must be removed from this area or he will worry too much about the work, or about you. At least from Calgary he can do nothing, and must get the rest he still very much needs.'

'But will everything be all right here if I leave for a week or more?' Kelly replied. 'I mean, Fred Griffiths is a fine cook and I believe he can handle the rest of it, but . . .'

'But you must go, and that is that,' was the blunt reply. 'If necessary I shall myself stay and keep order here, but first I think this man Griffiths deserves a chance. We are always needing good men who can run a camp properly. Come, we will go and see him now, so that you can begin your preparations for the trip.'

They spent the remainder of the day sorting out the various aspects of the takeover, and with her own nerves jangling from her latest encounter with Grey Scofield, Kelly was increasingly pleased at Marcel's matter-of-fact approach to the problem. His volatile personality and Gallic courtliness were soothing to her ego and her own flash-point temper.

After a dinner in which Marcel united with Fred Griffiths to introduce a mildly unusual menu for the evening, Marcel took Kelly by the arm and insisted gently that they wander down by the river so that she could try to relax.

'You are letting Scofield upset you far too much,' he said. 'So you must go with him to Calgary—so what? Your father is with you, and Scofield's mother, who must be a most formidable woman to have raised such a son. In truth, I would come with you myself, but that is for the moment impossible. But it is nothing to worry about.'

He turned the conversation to other, more pleasant topics, and by the time sunset began to pool shadows against the vivid colours of the sky, Kelly was more at ease than she had been in weeks. They strolled hand-in-hand beside the river, Marcel courting her with a widespread frivolity that was more comforting than erotic, and Kelly found herself responding with a flirtatious pleasure that was enhanced by the lack of seriousness.

Only when they returned to her trailer did Marcel reveal that his flirting was not as lighthearted as she had imagined.

Raising her fingers to his lips, he kissed them with an intensity that was far from the formal gesture she had expected, and seconds later he was pulling her into his embrace as his lips sought her own amidst a barrage of endearments.

Surprised, but not really put off by the embrace, Kelly raised her lips to meet his, and felt his arms close around her with unexpected gentleness. It was a pleasant, comfortable, but uninspiring kiss, fired by Marcel's passion, but equally cooled by the lack of a responding passion from Kelly herself.

She couldn't help the immediate comparison with the soul-destroying kisses of Grey Scofield, whose lips seemed to light her every nerve even when she was angry with him.

Marcel kissed her a second time, then slowly released her as his awareness of her cool response became more acute. His fingers slid away from her shoulders with a tangible sadness, and she could see in his eyes the knowledge that her heart was already enslaved somewhere else.

'I see——' he began, but before he could continue the sound of approaching footsteps in the gravel made both of them turn to face the intruder.

Grey's eyes were cold with barely suppressed anger as he halted, hands on hips, and stared down at Kelly. He ignored Marcel so completely, so arrogantly, that the French-Canadian might as well not have existed.

'Sorry to interrupt,' growled that gravelly voice. 'But I'm leaving at five in the morning. If you're coming, you'd maybe better think about getting some sleep.'

Kelly's whispered reply was wasted upon his broad back as he turned and strode away without waiting for an answer or deigning to speak to Marcel, who muttered something foul in gutter French as Grey disappeared into the darkness.

Kelly waited to hear no more. Muttering a brief goodnight to Marcel, she fled into the sanctuary of her trailer, where she sat awake for long hours and wondered how she could possibly bear to spend a week in the company of a man who so obviously despised her. When she finally did fall asleep, it was to turn and stretch restlessly throughout the short remainder of the night.

Morning arrived with no solution to her problems. It took only moments to pack a small case; the best of her clothing was in Grande Prairie and would have to be picked up en route. Kelly looked into her mirror and was unimpressed by the red-rimmed eyes with dark circles beneath them. It took the best of her make-up skills to repair her appearance so as not to cause her father undue worry when they arrived to collect him.

Promptly at five o'clock, she closed the trailer door and sat down on the step outside to await Grey. It was only a minute before he approached her, stepping out in his distinctive, long-legged stride.

'Is this all you're taking?' he asked brusquely, reaching down to pick up her small overnight case.

'My better clothes are in town,' she replied with equal abruptness. His only reply was a grunt of assent as he handed her into the truck, threw the case on to her lap and walked quickly around to seat himself behind the steering wheel.

They drove from the camp in a hostile silence that seemed to deepen with each passing mile. Down across Mouse Cache Creek, through the close-mowed airstrip at Sherman Meadows and finally to the mist-shrouded waters of the south lake at Two Lakes—the truck rumbled its way over the dusty gravel track and its occupants stared straight ahead in total, chilling silence.

But as they swung around the bend to come in sight of the north lake, a flicker of movement beside the road caught Kelly's eye and she gasped with amazement a second later.

'Oh . . . oh, Grey, stop! Please stop,' she cried involuntarily as a big cow moose, her gangling, wobbly-legged calf at foot, splashed from the marsh at the lake shore and trotted almost directly towards the truck. There are few animals so hopelessly clumsy-looking and yet strangely appealing as young moose, and to Kelly, who had never seen one before of that age, it was a sight to be savoured. As the truck slowed to a halt, she rolled down her side window and stuck her head out to watch with delight as the long-legged calf floundered along behind its mother.

Kelly watched until both animals had crossed the road, then turned to find Grey watching her with gentle amusement in his eyes. 'Wasn't it absolutely delightful?' she cried excitedly, forgetting in her own pleasure that they were supposed to be angry with one another.

'It was indeed,' he replied gravely, reaching down to thrust the truck into gear again so they could resume their journey.

'You think I'm silly, don't you?' Kelly demanded. She was quite unashamed of her enthusiasm, and was angered that Grey might think it childish.

'Only when you make remarks like that,' he growled. 'There's nothing silly about enjoying the sight of a wild animal like that. I enjoyed it just as much as you did, if not quite so noisily, and I've seen it many, many times before.'

Kelly didn't know what to reply, and they continued along in silence for a few minutes. Suddenly, however, Grey flung the truck up on to the verge and turned off the ignition as he turned to face Kelly.

'Look, before we get to town I think it's best we have a bit of a chat,' he said seriously. 'We're going to be spending the next week in rather close proximity and I don't really want all this antagonism to upset your father.'

'Well, neither do I,' said Kelly, then refrained from adding that it hadn't been she who had started it.

'Good. We'll call a truce then?' Grey looked unduly solemn as he reached out his hand. Kelly looked at it cautiously.

'I'm not sure,' she said, 'that we'll be able to stick to it unless you promise to keep your hands to yourself. I've had quite enough of being mauled by you every time you want to make some point or another.'

'Damn it, woman, shaking hands is hardly a prelude to mauling,' he grumbled, looking at his own palm as if expecting to find it covered in grease.

'Okay. Truce it is,' said Kelly, reaching out her own tiny hand and placing it in his. Just the touch was enough to send shivers up her spine, and when he clasped his fingers around her hand for an instant before releasing it, she had to restrain a visible shudder of delight.

Grey started up the truck again, and they drove for some time without speaking. But now the silence was far less hostile than before; it was almost, Kelly thought to herself, comfortable.

Looking sideways, her glance hidden by long lashes, she could surreptitiously study Grey's strong, intensely masculine profile and the easy movement of his hands on the wheel of the truck. In tight whipcord trousers, the flexing muscles of his thigh were all too evident as he shifted through the gears on the rising and falling roadway.

'Acually, you know, there are times when I rather like you.' The comment was so sudden, so totally unexpected, that Kelly flinched at the sound. And having flinched, she could think of no truly suitable reply.

'Don't you want to know what those times are?' Grey asked after a further long silence. He didn't take his eyes from the road, but Kelly sensed he was watching her reaction from the corner of his vision.

'I'd be more interested to know why you've never shown it,' she finally replied, and instantly regretted the flippant tone.

'Probably because they're so rare they surprise me,' he replied calmly, 'and if it's any help to you, they *don't* include the times you want to be a smarty-pants with that rapier tongue of yours.'

He was grinning just slightly, and Kelly found herself falling into something of his bantering mood.

'It's hardly my fault you expect all women to be awed into silence by your very presence,' she retorted saucily.

Grey laughed aloud, his voice booming through the relatively small enclosure of the truck cab. 'It's been my experience that women are always odd but seldom silent,' he replied, then chuckled again as Kelly giggled at his deliberate play on words.

'Very well,' she said at last, 'so just exactly when are these rare moments when I meet with your approval? When I'm cooking, I suppose?'

'A cook of your calibre is a treasure in itself,' Grey replied, 'but I was thinking more of times like when we saw the little moose calf, and the odd time I've seen you watching the sunset and really *seeing* it.'

Kelly didn't know what she might reply to that comment, so she kept silent, and Grey also fell into a calm, serene quiet that lasted almost until they reached the Wapiti bridge on the southern outskirts of the city.

'Your father's liable to balk rather considerably when we spring this Calgary thing on him,' Grey said then. 'Can I count on your support? I'll need it, because he can be stubborn as a mule when he sets his mind to it.'

Kelly was aghast. 'Do you mean you haven't even told him?' she demanded. 'The way you brought it up I thought it was all arranged.'

'It is. I just haven't told him yet,' Grey replied. 'To be honest, I wanted to have you on my side first.'

'Well, you would certainly have done better to come out with the truth in the first place,' she retorted. 'If it wasn't for the fact that Marcel agrees with you, I'm not sure that I would, regardless of the arguments.'

'So old Marcel agrees with me, hey? That's a first, I can tell you,' said Grey.

'So I should imagine,' Kelly replied. 'And he's not *old*; I imagine he's actually younger than you are.'

'There are times when I think *everybody* is younger than I am,' Grey replied with a cynical tone. 'And other times when I'm sure of it.'

'How awful for you,' she said rather tartly.

'Oh, it isn't too bad really; some girls prefer older men,' he grinned. 'I take it that I can count on your support with papa bear?'

'Yes, you can,' Kelly admitted. 'Although I'm still not sure that I should be going along. I don't really feel I deserve the holiday, and if my father and your . . . your mother are old friends as you say, I can't see that he really needs my moral support.'

'Probably doesn't, but I would like you to meet dear old Mom. You'll probably get on like a house on fire; she's got a rougher tongue even than you have.'

Kelly didn't bother to pick up that challenge; she was too busy wondering about the implications of meeting Grey's mother. Why? She worried at it like a dog with a bone, but could see no truly logical answer.

As Grey had predicted, Geoff Barnes raised a howl of protest at the prospect of being sent to Calgary as an invalid. But in the face of what appeared on the surface to be a united front, he finally backed down and agreed that the rest would be pleasant.

Still, he groused about it all the way back to the house, where Kelly insisted he sit down and rest while she packed the necessary clothing and accessories for both of them. Grey, who required a minimum of packing because he obviously kept clothes at his Calgary home, wandered into Kelly's room as she was looking over her dresses and wondering what to pack.

'Bring along that checked dress,' he said without preamble. 'And the green dress too; we aren't terribly formal, but Mom likes to dress up for dinner.'

Kelly was first inclined to take neither dress, just to spite him, but as he maintained his lounging position just inside the doorway, she chose instead to ignore his presence as she carefully folded both dresses into her suitcase.

'Is it all right with Your Majesty if I wear this to travel in?' she queried lightly, indicating her pale green jumpsuit. 'Or do you think the airline crew would expect something more feminine?'

'The captain definitely would, but I guess it wouldn't accomplish much since he'll be too busy flying to pay that much attention,' he replied with his normal mocking grin. 'It wouldn't do to have the poor fellow all hot and bothered while he's flying.'

It wasn't until they arrived at the airport that Kelly caught the true import of that comment. Instead of the commercial terminal, Grey turned his truck towards a small private hangar, where a crew was already preparing a private aircraft.

'Oh,' Kelly muttered half to herself, and Grey turned to regard her with a slight smile.

'Surprised?' he said. 'Don't worry about it, dear girl, I'm

actually a fairly good pilot. Haven't killed anybody yet, at any rate.'

'It's just that I've never flown in a small aircraft before,' she replied. 'I'm rather looking forward to it, as a matter of fact.'

'Well, if you're especially good I might let you have a go at flying it yourself,' he said, handing her father up into the main passenger compartment and then lifting in the various articles of luggage. It seemed obvious that he expected Kelly to share the cockpit with him, and she was standing, waiting for him to open it, when a blaring car horn announced the arrival of a speeding taxi.

'Grey, darling!' came a voice from the passenger seat. 'Oh, how lucky I caught you! Now I can catch a lift south with you and not have to endure the utter boredom of the commercial flights.'

Even as Grey and Kelly turned, the door flung open to allow Freda Jorgensen to alight, and she strode towards them as the taxi driver began unloading her luggage.

Freda was dressed in what some people would have considered casual gear, but the expense of it took the clothing well out of Kelly's conception of casual. The black, velvet-textured slacks, fitting almost like a second skin, revealed a figure of startling attractiveness, and the creamy blouse that so perfectly matched the woman's white-blonde hair was open low enough to reveal the swellings of a high, firm bosom. Freda's handbag had cost more than Kelly's entire set of luggage, and her shoes were a light, decorative wonder compared with Kelly's stout walking shoes.

Freda didn't bother with any more than perfunctory greetings, but immediately positioned herself so as to join Grey in the cockpit. Kelly, hoping for just an instant that he would recall his promise of only moments before, waited only a moment before admitting defeat and scrambling in to join her father in the rear compartment.

From that moment, what should have been an exciting and wonderful journey turned into a private hell. From their position in the rear, Kelly couldn't avoid seeing Freda's carefully manicured fingers playing along Grey's thigh muscles as he manipulated the aircraft, and the woman's tinkling laugh and intense, obviously private comments chilled Kelly's own feelings into a solid lump of ice.

It was left to her father to direct Kelly's attention to the various sights as they flew south-east on a long diagonal that parallelled the magnificence of the Rocky Mountains. They crossed the headwaters of the Athabasca, the Saskatchewan, the Brazeau and the Clearwater rivers, flying the boundaries of Jasper and Banff National Parks on their way south.

From Kelly's position on the right-hand side of the aircraft, she was exposed to some of the most beautiful mountain scenery in the world. Tall peaks, some of them still covered in caps of glistening snow, loomed like a fortress against the sky, with here and there the flashing gleam of a high waterfall, and the sheen of a glass-clear mountain stream. The lower foothills beneath them were cloaked in the dark, black-green hues of pine and spruce forests, giving way to the lighter green of the alpine meadows at the higher elevations.

'Coming back, I'll try and have Grey fly over Kakwa camp so you can see it all from the air,' Geoff Barnes told his daughter, but while Kelly smiled her approval it was a false, hollow smile. The arrival of Freda Jorgensen had cast a pall over her entire existence, and all Kelly really wanted was for the trip to end, so that she could free herself from the presence of both the blonde beauty and Grey Scofield himself.

The spires of Calgary's city centre were tall on their left when Grey finally began to bring the aircraft lower, and Kelly realised he wasn't aiming for the city or its airport, but for a private landing strip on a site several miles south and west of Calgary.

A large, gleaming station wagon was waiting as they taxied to a halt, and Kelly wasn't surprised when Freda was carefully handed into the front passenger seat beside Grey. The man who had brought the vehicle waved cheerfully to them before walking off to attend to the aircraft, and Kelly presumed someone would be sent later to pick him up.

Freda Jorgensen chatted gaily as they drove towards the distant ranch headquarters, pointedly ignoring Kelly and her father as if she were alone in the car with Grey. To Kelly, it seemed the other woman was over-particular in establishing Grey's plans for the visit, and was obviously planning to pre-empt as much of his time as possible.

The ranch-house was a huge, sprawling, single-storey structure that formed a broad U around a courtyard housing a glassed-in swimming pool, with ranks of stables and outbuildings partway down the rise behind the main house. As Grey steered the station wagon in under a carport at the end of the building, a tall, slender woman strode around the corner to meet them as they alighted.

'Geoff! You hardly look like the invalid I expected,' she cried in a rich, musical voice as she hugged Kelly's father to her and kissed him gently on the cheek.

'I started getting better the minute they said you were going to be my nurse, Meg,' Geoff Barnes responded with a broad grin. 'Having time to spend with both you and Kelly would make any man feel healthy.'

'And so it should,' she replied, speaking over her shoulder as she turned to greet Kelly with an outstretched hand and welcoming smile. 'You're much prettier than any of your pictures, my dear,' Margaret Scofield said. 'I can see why Grey has spent so much time in camp recently.'

Kelly, unsure how to reply to so provocative a statement, only smiled her own greetings. She was too aware of

Grey—and Freda—standing just behind her.

There was no attempt made to introduce Freda to Grey's mother, and Kelly assumed they must know each other, especially when Grey began to speak.

'I'll just unload this luggage and then let you get these people settled, Mom,' he said after kissing his mother fleetingly on one cheek. 'I'll run Freda into town and be back in time for lunch.'

'Oh, but there is no need,' the blonde interrupted. 'I can just telephone my papa and he will come for me, or send a car at least.' It was clear that she was angling for a luncheon invitation, but to Kelly's surprise Grey didn't take it up.

'Waste of time,' he replied briskly. 'I have things to do anyway in town, and your father has better things to do than play chauffeur to you, young miss.'

And with no room for argument, he hefted out Kelly and Geoff Barnes' suitcases and handed Freda back into the station wagon before she could possibly object.

'You'll want a drink first, I suppose,' Meg Scofield said to Kelly's father, waving aside his attempt to carry in the bags. 'Leave those; I'll have them brought in. You're supposed to be sick, remember? Tell me, Kelly, is he allowed a drink, or should we stick him right back into bed with a good book?'

Both women had to laugh at Geoff's expression of outrage at the suggestion, and a moment later they were comfortably seated in the huge living room, glasses in hand.

Despite Geoff Barnes' protestations, he was obviously tired by the journey, and after one drink he grudgingly admitted that a nap before lunch might be welcome. Kelly's restlessness of the night before had caught up with her, and she too agreed to the suggestion.

The room to which she was shown had a bathroom en suite, and a set of sliding glass doors provided access to the covered, heated pool outside. Kelly lay down on the broad double bed, visibly weary but unsure if she would be able to rest. She closed her eyes just for a moment and opened them in startled surprise when a thunderous knocking at her door and an all-too-familiar gravel voice announced that she would be late for lunch if she didn't hurry.

'I'll only be a minute,' she replied hastily, springing up from the bed and rushing towards the bathroom. Her first thought was the tumbled mane of her hair, but Kelly knew also that her eyes would reveal the tensions within her if she didn't use careful judgment with her make-up.

'Don't panic,' growled the voice. 'Actually, I lied just a touch. You've got at least half an hour yet. What I really wondered was if you'd like a swim first.'

'Oh, I don't think so,' she replied, already reaching for her hairbrush. 'I didn't bring a swimsuit with me.'

'Use this,' Grey replied, and the door opened just enough for him to throw in a few wisps of cloth before closing it again.

Kelly picked up the tiny bikini, eyes widening at the skimpiness of it. Surely he didn't expect her to swim in this!

'It doesn't, you know,' he said through the door, his voice now soft enough that only Kelly could hear.

'Doesn't what?' she replied without thinking, her mind racing at the daring she would need to wear such a flimsy swimsuit even in a private pool.

'It doesn't belong to who you think,' he growled. 'So with that excuse out of the way, there's only modesty to fall back on . . . or are you just going to admit you're a prude?'

'I am not!' Kelly snapped out the answer without really considering it, and instantly regretted her quick tongue.

'Good. I'll meet you in the pool, then,' he said with a tangible hint of satisfaction evident in his voice.

Kelly shrugged off her jump-suit and slipped into the wispy, pale green fabric of the minuscule bikini. The full-length mirror in the bathroom was tempting, but she forced herself not to take advantage of it, afraid that if she were faced with the visible evidence of the bikini's skimpiness, she would never dare to wear it.

Instead, she slid open the glass doors and walked slowly towards the edge of the pool, feeling horribly fragile and exposed. Her father's appreciative whistle from a poolside lounge chair did little for her confidence, though she threw him a slightly abashed grin in return.

'Well, well, well! Fits better than I thought,' came Grey's voice from behind her, but before Kelly could turn she was hoisted skyward like a child in his strong hands.

'Let's see how it washes,' he laughed, and ignoring her shriek of anticipation he threw her bodily into the sparkling water and dived in right behind her. As Kelly surfaced, spluttering with indignation, a cap of silver reared from the water right before her and she was faced with Grey's cheerful, mocking grin.

'You . . . you . . .' she spluttered, then clenched her teeth and thrust both hands forward to smother his face in a wave of spray. Since he was opening his mouth to speak just as she splashed him, Grey received a proper mouthful of water and did some spluttering of his own before he reared out of the water like some great silver-haired seal and reached out to grasp at Kelly's arms.

She was too quick, however, and had already turned to begin swimming frantically for the side. She felt his fingers graze across her ankle as she kicked away, and the touch was like a brand despite the cool comfort of the water.

Grey was a smooth and powerful swimmer, and as Kelly touched the edge of the pool he surfaced beside her and slid up on to the tiled rim, reaching down to offer his hand.

'You swim well,' he grinned, and his enthusiasm was so obviously genuine that she felt her initial anger dissipate. She allowed Grey to hand her out of the pool, then turned and dived back in beside him, churning the water frantically as she raced him towards the far end and back again. She lost by a wide margin.

'Have to do better than that, Kelly,' her father called from his lounge chair, but Kelly barely heard. She was all too conscious of her bosom heaving beneath the flimsy swimsuit as Grey once again leaned down to help her from the water.

The upper half of Grey's muscular body was deeply tanned, with only a slightly visible line showing the still darker hue of his forearms and throat. He must work without a shirt for most of the summer, she thought, an impression confirmed when she glanced down at sturdy legs that were almost as pale as her own.

Grey handed her a towel, then turned to her father. 'She'll never be a swimming racer, Geoff,' he laughed. 'Not with those little feet.' He held one of his own feet out for inspection and continued, 'By comparison I might as well be wearing swim fins; it's just no contest.'

'I'll bet you snowshoe race without snowshoes, too,' Kelly responded tartly, although she matched his grin with one of her own. She found Grey's good humour—at least in the absence of Freda Jorgensen—exceptionally infectious.

'I take any advantage I can,' he replied with a grim stare that was obvious only to Kelly, and his look was a warning she was clearly meant to see. Any responsibility for a reply was lost when Grey's mother arrived to announce that lunch was ready, and Kelly thankfully fled to her room to slip into a robe and pull her soaked hair into a straggly ponytail.

When she entered the patio, Grey rose gracefully to his feet to seat her, and to her astonishment complimented her on the hair-do. 'It was like that—sort of—the first time I saw you,' he grinned. 'Looked a little better dry, of course, but the effect is the same. You look about fifteen.'

'Which is nothing to complain about,' his mother interjected. 'We women grow old soon enough as it is.'

To Kelly's surprise, Grey responded with a harsh laugh. 'You'll never look old,' he told his mother with a chuckle of inner satisfaction. 'And telling everybody it was me that

turned you grey at twenty-three isn't going to make a single
bit of difference, because I can always say—quite
honestly—that you made *me* grey twice.'

He turned to look at Kelly's wondering expression.
'Once at only two days old, if you please,' he explained,
'and if that wasn't bad enough she did it again when I was
only eighteen. It's enough to put me off women for life!'

Geoff Barnes and Kelly laughed at the deliberate play on
words, but Margaret Scofield merely shook her head sadly.
'You're right about the first time,' she replied, 'but you
should be thankful for inheriting my premature grey hair.
You might have taken after your father, don't forget; he
was *bald* at thirty.'

'Some women think baldness is a sign of virility,' he
replied saucily, then rubbed his palm across the silver
waves of his hair. 'All this does is make them all think I'm
too old for them. Kelly's been avoiding me for that reason
ever since she arrived, haven't you, my child?'

The question caught Kelly slightly off guard, and she
struggled momentarily for an answer before Grey interrupted.

'Or was it that you preferred old men?' he asked with a
deliberate and mischievous grin.

This time she was ready for him. 'Oh, I was interested
for a moment,' she replied, 'until I found out that Freda
wasn't your daughter, as I'd suspected.'

The acid reply brought whoops of laughter from the two
parents, but although Grey seemed to join in it, his eyes
burned at Kelly with a strange intensity and foreboding.

'That was a low blow, Miss Barnes,' he replied, and then
countered by relating his first meeting with Kelly and his
belief at the time that she was a misguided student radical.
'. . . The proof that first impressions can be misleading, but
she still refuses me the same courtesy,' he concluded mean-
ingfully.

His expression warned Kelly that she'd not heard the

last of his anger, and when he suddenly rose and excused himself on the promise of urgent business in the city, she knew he wasn't being entirely truthful.

He strode off to change, leaving Kelly to sit in mild exasperation as her father and Grey's mother exchanged meaningful glances.

'It's rude of me to ask, I suppose,' Meg Scofield said after Grey had repeated his farewell and left the house, 'but have you two been sniping at each other like this from the very beginning?'

'More or less,' Kelly admitted with a shy glance at her father. She was afraid of upsetting him, but the burst of laughter he emitted at her hedging comment showed she was fooling nobody.

'They think they're so smart,' Geoff Barnes chuckled. 'Reckon an old man in a hospital is stupid as well as sick, but they forgot I have eyes as good as the next man's. You've got something going for Grey, haven't you, Kelly?'

'Indeed I have,' she replied flippantly despite the surge of emotion the comment generated. 'I think it's called a personality clash in some circles. No offence, Mrs Scofield, but I find your son to be the most stubborn, opinionated and domineering man I've ever met.'

'Well, I should certainly hope so,' came the unexpected reply. 'Although I must admit he has a way to go before he's as good as his father. Oh, I wish you could have met him, Kelly. He and I fought from the very beginning. It didn't matter who was present and it seldom mattered who was right, all it needed was for Greyson and me to be in the same room and the fireworks started. My own father said the only reason he allowed the marriage was because it was a shame to spoil two houses with us.'

'Ignoring, of course, the fact that he couldn't have stopped you,' Kelly's father interrupted with a chuckle. 'All the fuss and fury wasn't on your husband's side, Meg, and you know it. I think your poor old dad was happy just to get rid of you.'

Margaret Scofield returned the comment with an accusation of her own, and minutes later the two of them were embroiled in a half friendly, half angry row that left Kelly totally in the background and increasingly concerned for her father's well-being. She sat in stunned amazement as they fought, watching the insults and accusations fly back and forth across the room with increasingly velocity until suddenly Geoff Barnes threw up his hands in a gesture of defeat.

'Enough, woman!' he roared in obvious exasperation. 'You're too much for me in my weakened condition, but give me a few days' rest and I'll paddle your bottom for you if that's what it takes to win.'

'You and whose army?' Meg snapped back with a jeering laugh. 'You're a guest in my home and don't you forget it, Geoffrey Barnes. Which means you'll do as I say—and I say it's time for you to take that poor, weary, tired *old* body off to bed before you collapse from old age and senility. Now!'

To Kelly's surprise, he accepted without any objection, pausing only to kiss Kelly lightly on the cheek as he passed and then to throw a kiss and a saucy wink at his hostess.

'Don't try and read too much into that little performance,' Meg warned Kelly quite seriously after Kelly's father was safely out of earshot. 'Your father and I are the best of friends and that's all there is to it. He fights with me because he knows I need it and because Grey, bless his soul, won't do it. And I fight with him because I need it and because we both enjoy it, but neither of us is fooling anybody; there isn't a bit of romance in it . . . just friendship.'

'Oh, but I wasn't . . .'

'Of course you weren't. And don't. With all due respect to your father, there isn't any man for me now that Greyson is gone and there won't be. And I'm sure you're aware that your dad's in much the same boat.'

'My . . . er . . . mother, you mean?'

Meg Scofield shrugged enigmatically. 'He's a one-woman man. The best kind there is.'

'But . . .' Kelly was honestly astounded. She had known her father only through his infrequent visits during her childhood, and although he had never in any way attempted to come between her and her mother, he had also never made any attempt she could see to effect a reconciliation. Her mother, indeed, had always made it abundantly clear that such a thing would be impossible in any event.

'You're wondering about him and your mother,' Meg replied as if Kelly hadn't even tried to interrupt. 'Your father's no fool, Kelly. He knew the first time she left him that he couldn't hold her, and I think he knew that the kind of love he felt wasn't being returned. But it couldn't stop him loving her, and I break no secrets in saying he's loved her all these years. It's too bad the way it worked out, but any woman who expects to change a man's entire way of life by marrying him is a damned fool . . . no offence to your mother.'

Meg shook her mane of silvery hair impatiently. 'Oh, maybe I'm just too old-fashioned. Certainly I lose patience with this modern concept of women's liberation. Grey's father gave me so much, but the concept of being liberated simply wasn't a part of our relationship. He was the strong one . . . in my eyes, and yet I know that in his eyes I was just as dominant a figure. We just . . . complemented each other's strengths and weaknesses, I guess.'

She paused to light a cigarette and then looked at Kelly with almost an assessing gleam in her eyes. 'Grey gets more like his father every day. I wouldn't want to see him marry the wrong woman through sheer stubbornness.'

The tall, grey-haired woman rose abruptly then and left the room without any attempt to explain her meaning. It was a departure that seemed almost rude, yet Kelly sensed there was no rudeness intended; Meg Scofield was close to overcome by the intensity of her own emotions, and had hidden them almost too well.

But what had she meant? Kelly threw off her robe and slid into the warm cosiness of the swimming pool, floating on her back and staring up at the swift-running clouds as she pondered the statement. Had Meg been warning Kelly off her son? Or was it a more subtle warning? Certainly the intentions of the blonde Freda Jorgensen were obvious enough . . . was Kelly being warned not to interfere?

If nothing else, it's a bit late to be warning me to watch my own feelings, Kelly thought to herself. Much, much too late. Worse, she realised that she—like her father—would only be able to love once. No second-best would suffice. And Grey Scofield was her choice, no question any longer about that.

Was this, then, the substance of Meg Scofield's hinted warning? The knowledge that Kelly was a one-man woman—coupled with the knowledge that Meg's son was already spoken for—by Freda Jorgensen? The thought was too dreadful to maintain, yet Kelly couldn't force it from her mind no matter how she tried. Suddenly the warm waters of the pool were soul-chilling, and she shivered into her robe and fled to her room. It would take all of her inner strength to endure a week in Grey Scofield's company, and once again Kelly wished she had never come.

CHAPTER SEVEN

KELLY's misgivings slid into the background during the following three days, days in which she hardly saw Grey. Rising before dawn, he was usually gone from the house before Kelly was even awake, and when he came home at all, it was in the small hours of the morning.

On the fourth day the pattern changed. Kelly rose fairly early herself, and slid open the door to the swimming pool area as she prepared for a long before-breakfast swim. She was wearing the bikini Grey had found for her so many days before, despite having occasionally thought she ought to go into the city and buy one of her own.

Sliding off her towelling robe, she dived cleanly into the cool, refreshing water, surfacing with a start as she suddenly realised she wasn't alone.

'Morning,' Grey drawled with a broad smile of welcome. His silvery hair glistened in the strengthening sunlight, and droplets of water gleamed from his dark-tanned body.

'Good morning,' Kelly replied, suddenly quite unsure of what else she might say. Just the sight of his lean, muscular body brought spasms of desire to her own slim figure, and her mouth was dry with emotion.

'I'm sort of a stranger here, but I have the weirdest feeling we've met before,' he said confidingly, and Kelly felt her heart leap. He wasn't angry with her any longer.

'I'm not sure,' she replied with a shy grin. 'But you do seem vaguely familiar. Are you by any chance related to the resident ghost?'

Grey's own surprise and bewilderment were obvious. 'Resident ghost? I'm afraid I don't understand.'

'Oh, it's probably just my imagination,' she replied. 'But there's this vague figure that sometimes stalks the halls of the place during the wee small hours. Of course it's always gone when I'm awake, but . . .'

'Oh, that ghost,' he interrupted. 'Yes, you might say I'm related. That was the ghost of too damned much business, which makes Jack a dull lad indeed. I think actually he's disappeared for the moment, and certainly I'm not very ghost-like, am I?'

He reached through the water and took her hand, placing it gently against his shoulder. Kelly didn't so much as think of resisting the gesture, and her fingers played softly along his collarbone in an orgy of examination that left her breath short.

'No,' she agreed. 'You're . . . quite substantial.'

'Did you miss me?'

The question was so totally unexpected that she almost answered it without thinking. Miss you? I've missed you more than you must ever know, she thought. 'Not really; was I supposed to?'

'Well, it wasn't part of any great plan or anything,' he replied. 'It's just that I remember explaining this trip as a holiday and it's been just about anything but.'

'Oh, but I've been having a most restful time,' she said innocently. 'I've been spending all my time with Father, which was the whole idea, I thought.'

'Not exactly the whole idea,' Grey replied. 'I had planned originally that you'd spend some time with me as well, but so far business matters have made a great hash of that idea.'

'Well, of course business must come first . . .'

'But not always,' Grey interrupted harshly, reaching out to capture her hand once again. 'And I've missed you, even if it hasn't been reciprocated.'

Kelly's heart fluttered at the possibility. Had he missed her? Had he even thought of her? Or had his *business* really revolved around the blonde attractions of Freda Jorgensen? Either way, there was no satisfactory answer to his implied question, and Kelly was saved by the timely arrival of her father.

'You both look bright and chipper this morning,' Geoff Barnes greeted them as he eased himself into the pool. He was improving every day, but still found himself so easily weakened by any form of exercise that he was taking things very carefully.

The sound of his voice caused Kelly to spin away from Grey in an automatic selfconscious movement, but the silver-haired figure reached out to reclaim her hand even as she bade her father good morning.

'We were just discussing what to do today,' Grey said. 'I presume you won't mind me taking Kelly away from her nursemaid duties?'

'Mind? I'd welcome it,' Geoff Barnes replied. 'Having her fluttering around like an amateur Florence Nightingale is enough to drive a man barmy. She'll have me thinking I'm sicker than I really am, if I let her.'

'Well, I like that!' Kelly retorted, surreptitiously trying to free her hand from Grey's grasp. 'If this is how you react to my concern, I might as well have stayed in Kakwa camp. The way you've been acting since we got here, I almost wonder if your entire illness hasn't been a sham.'

'That's no way to speak to a sick man, and even less to your father,' Geoff Barnes replied with a half-amused grin. 'And if you two want to cuddle, perhaps you'd be so kind as to move to one side so that I have room to swim.'

Kelly stood, her mouth open in shocked outrage, while Grey reached out his arm to wrap it around her waist. 'You heard the man,' he chuckled in her ear. 'You wouldn't want to disobey your own father, would you?'

Her answer was a vicious backward elbow jab that forced a grunt of astonishment from him before she slipped from his arm and sped to the side of the pool.

'I think you're both quite hopeless,' she panted in mock anger after slithering out of the water scant inches ahead of Grey's fingers. 'It would serve you both right if I refused to cook you breakfast!'

Her father was instantly contrite, but Grey looked back with stubborn disdain. 'I was cooking my own breakfast when you were still in three-cornered pants, little girl,' he growled menacingly. 'That's one threat that doesn't hold much water.'

'Well, if you're so smart, you can prepare breakfast for all of us then,' Kelly retorted, turning on her heel to stalk back towards her room in what she hoped was a good imitation of high dudgeon. She wasn't really angry at all, and after drying her hair thoroughly, she slipped into jeans and a T-shirt and wandered out to the kitchen.

She was cracking the first egg over a slow pan when Grey, casually dressed in a pair of much-faded denims and soft Indian moccasins but still shirtless, strode into the room and grasped her wrist.

'I thought I was delegated to be cook,' he said accusingly.

'What are we supposed to do, starve to death while we wait for you?' Kelly replied. 'It'll be bad enough being restricted to toast and coffee, I should imagine.'

'Get your butt out of here, woman of little faith,' he growled in reply, turning her round and snacking her none too gently across the seat of her jeans. Her squeal of surprise cut across the morning greetings of Meg Scofield, who had come in just in time to view the byplay.

'I do wish you children wouldn't play in the kitchen,' Mrs Scofield chided in a tone so realistic she sounded actually serious. 'And there's no sense arguing with him, Kelly, he only sulks if he doesn't get his own way.' Taking Kelly by one arm, she steered her towards the door.

'I'll have crêpes Suzette, pork sausages, black coffee and three slices of light toast, dear,' she threw back over her shoulder. 'And please stop burning that egg.'

Grey looked back at the smouldering egg and threw a look of total frustration after the departing women. 'You'll have ham and eggs and damned well like it!' he shouted, and his mother looked down at Kelly with a friendly, conspiratorial chuckle.

'Sometimes it's best to keep them just a shade off balance,' she whispered, then raised her voice in cheerful greeting to Geoff Barnes.

Breakfast was better than Kelly had anticipated, although even as the thought crossed her mind she realised she had no basis for assuming Grey couldn't cook. They were settling down to final cups of rich, strong coffee when the subject of the day's activities was again raised.

'I think I'll take Kelly off to Banff for a few days,' Grey replied to a query from Geoff Barnes. 'If we stay around here that phone will be ringing with some emergency or another.'

Kelly tried to conceal her surprise. It was one thing to have him suggesting a few days away, but to have the suggestion emerge in front of their respective parents was a bit much, she thought. Or didn't Grey think they understood that a few days must by attrition include a few nights? Her own father had merely nodded as if it were the most common request in the world, but Grey's mother, thank heavens, was shaking her head in a negative gesture.

'Kelly, have you anything really striking to wear to a terribly posh party?' she asked, ignoring Grey's suggestion entirely.

Vaguely confused by the turnaround, Kelly shook her own head in negative reply. Even the best she had brought with her didn't qualify.

'Well then, Banff is definitely out,' the older woman replied. 'We shall have to spend at least this afternoon shopping, and perhaps tomorrow morning as well. And I shall have to get you an appointment tomorrow with my hairdresser.'

'Mother, what are you talking about?' Grey interrupted.

'Why, the Jorgensens' party tomorrow night, of course,' she replied calmly. 'Freda rang yesterday to remind me, and to extend an invitation to our guests. Naturally, I accepted.'

'Naturally,' Grey muttered with ill-disguised sarcasm.

'You know very well Sven would have been quite put out if you'd forgotten,' his mother replied. 'It's his birthday, and an annual party we haven't missed in years.'

Grey's face revealed his agreement, but Kelly's heart leaped at the thought that he might have actually forgotten the party in the enthusiasm of spending some time with her. His next words, however, dashed her feelings like a glass of ice water.

'I don't know how I managed to forget,' he muttered absently, 'Freda mentioned it to me herself just the other night.'

Just the other night? When he was supposedly *working*? Kelly's spirits fell like a stone at the thought of what kind of work Grey would be doing that involved Freda Jorgensen. She hardly heard Meg Scofield arranging for their shopping trip that morning, merely nodding agreement to whatever suggestion. It hardly seemed to matter any more.

'I think I'd better take Kelly.' Those words did penetrate her fog. Grey's voice was too distinctive and too imprinted on her to be missed.

'Oh no! I mean, it really isn't necessary,' she blurted. 'Surely one of the dresses I brought with me will suffice. I mean, there's no real reason for me to be too fancied up.'

'There is and they won't,' he growled, answering her objections with a distinctly high-handed tone of voice.

Kelly felt herself retreating in an almost physical gesture. She simply could not, would not, allow this arrogant man to take her shopping. Just the thought of it both terrified and angered her. How could he even suggest coming with them?

'Come if you like, but you can keep your opinion to

yourself until it's asked for,' Grey's mother answered for them, leaving Kelly's objections ignored.

And an hour later they were threading the large station wagon into downtown Calgary, where Grey quickly found a parking garage and blithely escorted both women out into the busy shopping centre.

He took one lady on each arm, striding briskly along as if shopping for women's clothes was the most natural activity in the world for him. Kelly, for her part, tried to free herself several times, but his grip was unassailable. By the time they reached the first exclusive dress shop, she was unaccountably flustered and indecisive.

With each dress she tried, Kelly grew more confused and angry, while Grey stood, silent, but his eyes spoke volumes as he solemnly observed each choice and turned thumbs down.

It was in the fourth, and most expensive shop that Kelly finally began to see some creations that suited her tiny figure and strong colouring. The best was a gauze-thin, starkly plain sheath of turquoise, which was to be worn under a caftan-style over-blouse that was a riot of shimmering, vibrant colour. When she tried it, mentally visualising her hair piled high and styled just right, Kelly knew this was the dress she wanted. Meg Scofield agreed, and Kelly tried to ignore Grey, not wanting to see his expression.

But she couldn't avoid it when she emerged from the changing room in what she mentally termed a second choice. This was a basic black, but a black gown that was so startlingly daring she knew she would never have the nerve to wear it anywhere. It stopped just short of being a peignoir, with only the gathering to compensate for the sheerness of the material. Revealing of bosom and thigh, shoulder and ankle, it required all Kelly's determination just to step out of the changing room in it.

'No!' The softly explosive whisper that shot from Grey's lips denied the look in his eyes, and Kelly looked through her own soft brown eyes to take in the flare of his nostrils and the tautness of his neck muscles.

No? How dared he? She swirled before the mirror, conscious of Grey's rigid stance as much as she was of his mother's questioning, high-arched brow. The dress was really not Kelly's style, although she knew at a glance it was exactly what Freda Jorgensen would wear, and carry it off with characteristic coolness as well.

Alone again in the dressing room, Kelly pondered Grey's vivid reaction at the same time as she pondered her finances. There was—barely—enough.

'I'll have them both,' she coolly told the startled sales assistant when she emerged a few moments later in her street clothes. It was a frightful extravagance, but to Kelly the look on Grey's face was almost compensation enough. His sharply indrawn breath during lunch when she confided to Meg Scofield that she would wear the black gown to the party was an added bonus with a bitter sweet, poignant flavour.

Kelly knew very well that she could never muster the nerve to wear the black gown in public. It would be difficult enough she thought, to wear it as the peignoir it so closely resembled, as a visual invitation and stimulant to a loved one. But Grey did not know it, and she planned to milk his ignorance for all the mileage she could.

Clearly he did not want her wearing that dress to the Jorgensen party, though for what reason Kelly couldn't quite imagine. Was it, perhaps, because Freda Jorgensen was likely to wear something similar, perhaps even something Grey had personally selected? His knowledge of women's fashions and the places they could be purchased displayed an unusual involvement in such things.

During the afternoon, spent purchasing the various accessories to complement both her gowns, Kelly was aware of Grey's distant, almost hostile disapproval whenever the black gown was displayed for comparisons and discussion. Not that he ever said anything; his expression was obvious enough.

She deliberately stayed close to her room the next morning, pleading organisational requirements as an excuse to keep from any confrontation with Grey, although in honesty she wasn't sure any such confrontation was in his plans.

In the afternoon, a lengthy visit to Mrs Scofield's hairdresser turned Kelly from ponytailed schoolgirl into a woman of maturity and distinction, yet somehow also managed to retain both her youth and innocence. Her long red hair was piled high in a vaguely Grecian styling, with small ringlets that emphasised the length and vulnerability of her slender neck. The judicious use of make-up and minimal jewellery would enhance the flowing lines of the high-collared caftan over-blouse, and since Kelly knew exactly what she was planning, she could discuss accessories for the black outfit with Meg Scofield during that evening's early tea with the easy knowledge that Grey would still not realise she had no intention of following through.

She returned to her room with an hour and a half in which to get ready—an hour more than Kelly had ever needed in her life—and was almost contemplating a brief nap when there was a soft knock at the door and it opened immediately to admit her host.

Kelly raised one eyebrow in silent query; they both knew why he was there, but she was determined not to be the first to mention it.

Grey's eyes raked briskly over Kelly's slender figure, resting briefly on the crowning glory of her hairdo, then he reached one hand from behind him to expose a small parcel wrapped in delicate floral paper.

'I should like you to wear this tonight, if you would,' he said in a voice that seemed velvet-soft.

Kelly smiled her thanks and turned to open the tiny

parcel, making slow work of it because her fingers trembled so. But finally she succeeded, to find a box containing a delicate, almost totally realistic flower. It was of raw silk, and obviously designed especially for the outfit she had chosen to wear that night. Tucked into her hair, it would make the perfect final accessory for the gown's swirls of gentle sea colour and vivid highlights.

With the black dress, it would look quite ridiculous.

'Oh, it's lovely!' Kelly breathed in honest admiration. 'But . . . but . . . . oh, Grey, I'm sorry. It just wouldn't go with that black dress.' No mention of the green; she didn't dare to bring it up, knowing that he had planned this particular present deliberately to force her to change her mind.

Grey's eyes seemed to grow wider, smouldering like the ashes that grow upon charcoal as it sears into flaming life that grows into the burning. Then they seemed to glaze over, taking a subtle dullness from the intensity of his carefully held-in anger.

'You're not really going to wear that black dress tonight.' He said it as a statement, with no hint of query. It was an aggressive, almost offensive denial of her right of choice.

'But of course. Why? Do you object?'

'You know damned well I do,' he growled, the anger escaping now like poorly-trapped steam.

Kelly lifted her small chin in obvious determination.

'Firstly,' she said, 'I don't see what business it is of yours *what* I wear. And secondly, I cannot imagine why you should object to the black dress. You said nothing at all when I bought it, not that I'd have listened anyway.'

'Exactly! But I'll damned well say something now. That dress is wrong for you. W.R.O.N.G. . . . wrong! It makes you look old and it makes you look . . .'

'It makes me look what?' Kelly's voice was almost a whisper as she tried to contain her own growing anger. She knew exactly what he meant; the dress would be perfect in the privacy of a love-nest, but in public—on Kelly—it teetered upon the brink of being expensively cheap. She lacked the cool sophistication that would allow Freda Jorgensen to wear such a gown with élan.

'It's too old for you,' Grey muttered half to himself.

'And so are you!' The timing was perfect, and his bronzed features went ashen with undisguised shock at the accusation. 'I don't need a father figure in you,' Kelly continued hurriedly before he could interrupt. 'I already have a father—and *he* doesn't tell me what to wear, either!'

'Well, he damned well should, and when he sees that dress he damned well will,' was the half-strangled reply. 'I just hope he paddles your pretty little rump for you while he's at it.'

'Get out!' The demand coincided with the smack of Kelly's small palm against Grey's cheek as her brown eyes blazed with anger.

Her wrist was clamped in an iron grasp as she swung her palm again, and she found herself meeting eyes like chips of grey ice. Grey was shaking his head angrily, oblivious to the angry palm mark upon his cheek. His jaw clenched as he forcibly restrained himself from returning her slap, and Kelly fiercely cried out her frustration.

'Why don't you hit me back? It would be just your style, wouldn't it? I shouldn't be able to attend the party with a black eye, should I? But I *would*! And I'd take the greatest of delight in telling everyone who hit me, too.'

'Even your father?' The question came too easily, too softly through the clenched teeth.

Kelly winced. Of course she couldn't tell her father Grey had struck her. And of course he couldn't strike her, either. Neither of them would risk Geoff Barnes' health or anger for the sake of their own bitter rage.

She yanked her hand away, pointing imperiously towards the door of her room. 'I shall wear what I choose,' she snarled. 'Now please leave.'

Grey was already turning towards the door when a sudden impulse made him turn instead to the closet where both gowns hung side by side.

His huge hand closed around the black gown on its hanger, lifting it from the closet in a swishing sound of sheer, feather-light gossamer. Kelly thought in sudden terror that he would rip the gown to shreds before her eyes, but instead he turned and threw it at her, hanger and all.

'Wear it and be damned,' he said, in a voice that was so deathly, frighteningly calm that Kelly reeled back from the frigid, tangibly icy anger in it.

Her fingers reached out to catch the gown as it struck her, and the folds of sheer black gauze floated up before her face like huge, inky wings, smothering in their softness. The chill of Grey's hostility seemed to transmit itself to the material itself, and Kelly almost dropped the gown again as her fingers felt the chill.

Before she could do that, much less speak, he was gone, and the door smashed itself futilely against the jamb with the fury of his passing.

She stood there, trembling, for several minutes. Then, staggering slightly, she moved to the closet and hung the dress up again before throwing herself face down on to her bed and fighting back the tears before they could surface.

She was, for a moment, successful. Then, singly, each tiny tear began its slow, uncertain journey down through the maze of her fists to the cover beneath. So much anger, so much hostility. And for what? To prove what? She would wear the dress that Grey preferred. She would even wear the tiny silk flower.

But neither, she knew, would reduce his antagonism in any useful way. At best, he would consider she had changed her mind as a measure of common sense. At worst, he would see it as a sign of submission, which was the last thing she wanted.

She would submit to him, to the love of him, but if that love were not returned he must never realise her own submission.

It took her extra care with her make-up to mask—as much as she could—the emotional turmoil within her, but Kelly still managed to leave her room spot on time for their departure.

She found Meg Scofield in the lounge room, swathed in a simple basic black gown that exactly suited the tall woman's erect carriage and dignified stature. Kelly's father strolled in a moment later, fingering awkwardly at his collar but looking splendid if slightly wan in his dinner suit. He let his eyes show his appreciation of both women while muttering mild curses about 'damned monkey suits' and slippery bow ties. Of Grey there was no sign.

'Grey has gone on ahead,' Mrs Scofield explained to a rather surprised Kelly. 'Something about business, he said, and it couldn't have been good if his expression meant anything.'

It was left to Geoff Barnes, under Meg's direction, to chauffeur them to the stately Jorgensen home. It was nearly seven miles away by road, but as Meg explained during the journey, corners of the two properties actually touched. 'If we drink too much we'll be able to walk home,' she laughed, realising full well that none of them would do any such thing.

Kelly's first impression of the Jorgensen home was one of amazement. It was huge, at least in appearance, and instead of blending with the surroundings as did Grey's home, it loomed and dominated like a mausoleum.

'Isn't it ridiculous?' Meg asked with a tinkling laugh. 'Grey always calls it "early Swedish awful", which upsets Freda no end.'

Able only to stare at the gargantuan structure, Kelly suddenly realised the true meaning of the term 'nouveau riche' in all of its bad-taste reality. The house was so hidous, so revoltingly awesome, that only a person of great personal insecurity would ever think of living in it. Certainly it didn't fit her assessment of Freda Jorgensen; could her father be so tremendously different than his chic, worldly daughter?

The man who greeted them inside the huge home was Kelly's first surprise of the party. Far from insecure, he was virtually the archetypal Nordic or Viking warrior. A huge man, blessed with a fiery red beard and only slightly less burnished hair, he loomed in the entry hall like a gigantic bear.

'Welcome, beautiful Meg,' he roared, hugging Grey's mother to him like a bear trying to climb a slender sapling. Then he released her after a hearty buss on the cheek, shook hands vigorously with Geoff Barnes, and turned upon Kelly with such vivid enthusiasm she almost flinched.

Enormous hands lifted her own as he planted kisses upon both her fingers and palms, having to bend almost double just to reach her. 'And to you, Miss Barnes, welcome to the ugliest house in the world,' he boomed. 'Ah, such hair! We must talk later, you and I. You are not yet married and I am a poor but honourable widower. You must consider me; with our hair we could produce absolutely astounding children.'

The sheer volume and overwhelming aliveness of the man followed them as he escorted them into the main hall of the home, where they received a substantially less warm welcome from Freda Jorgensen.

Or at least Kelly did. Geoff and Meg were hurried off to meet somebody Kelly had never heard of, and it was done in such a way that she was left standing alone at the edge of the huge room wondering at the ease with which it had all happened. Freda had come close to ignoring Kelly as if she didn't exist, and when she was still alone a few moments later, Kelly began to wonder if the other woman was a witch, and if she herself was now truly invisible.

Then she turned at a slight sound behind her and wondered if she were seeing things.

'Marcel!' she exclaimed with undisguised surprise. 'But . . . but what are *you* doing here?'

'I am thinking I have been invited as, what do you call it, a diversion,' he replied with surprising candour. 'You look wonderful, Kelly. I can see why the Viking princess arranged for me to be here.'

'*She* arranged it?' Kelly understood Marcel's comment well enough. What she doubted was the logic of what he seemed to be saying.

'Of course,' he replied. 'You have her just a teeny bit worried, little red fox, so she invited me here to try and draw you away from her own quarry, as it were. It would have been such a good plan, too, except that she doesn't know what you and I do.'

'You're teasing me,' Kelly replied shakily. How could she possibly pose any threat to the cool beauty of Freda Jorgensen? Marcel had to be joking, though she couldn't imagine why.

It was all too mystifying. Certainly Marcel looked utterly splendid in his rich evening clothes, indeed he outshone the various more citified men Kelly noticed around the room by his sheer physical size and pantherish movements. But what could Freda hope to gain by inviting him to this party? Did she plan to use Marcel to make Grey jealous? It was highly possible, since she was certainly in a position to understand that the two men didn't get on together. But if that were the case, why would she steer Marcel on to Kelly?

'I was clearly given to understand that I am to ensure you do not feel . . . lonely . . .' he said to her, steering her out into the throng of milling dancers. Kelly moved with him unquestioningly; there was so much she didn't understand about this situation, and neither Grey nor Freda seemed to be in evidence.

At one turn, they saw Kelly's father dancing slowly with Meg Scofield, but if Geoff Barnes saw anything strange in Marcel's presence at the party he gave no sign of it.

Kelly twirled happily enough in Marcel's arms. He was a marvellous dancer indeed, and after their last encounter in camp she knew he could only be a friend.

'You ... didn't exactly argue about coming here tonight, did you?' she asked with sudden inspiration, and was rewarded with a sly grin.

'*Moi*? Of course not,' he chuckled. 'Miss Freda is a bit ... er ... transparent to an old roué like me. She thinks that I fancy the little red fox for my own, so I am ... flattered ... by her confidence in me.'

He gave a short bark of typically Gallic laughter, then switched into soft French to explain his presence as much as he himself understood the situation.

Kelly had Freda Jorgensen just a bit worried, he said. Not terribly worried, but just a little. And since Freda imagined there might be something between him and Kelly, she had apparently decided Marcel might occupy Kelly sufficiently at the party to leave Freda a clear field with Grey.

'She is a fool,' he said vehemently. 'If she were just a little smarter she would have made the play for me herself. Your grey wolf, he dislikes me just enough that such a move might have gained her his undivided attention. This way, I think she defeats her own purpose. Grey will see you with me ... and poof! the blonde will disappear into the wallpaper, if such a thing is possible. *Mon Dieu!* Have you ever seen such an ugly house?'

He then turned to describing the house in such vivid gutter French that Kelly howled with laughter, and several other dancers threw strange looks in their direction. When the set was ended, Marcel steered her to a quiet corner and slipped away to find drinks for both of them, leaving her to contemplate the rather strange implications of his appearance at the party.

Fair enough, she thought, for Freda not to realise that she and Marcel had never been romantically involved, and that indeed they were closer to being true friends than lovers. But Kelly couldn't accept Marcel's presence in the simple terms that he himself did. It made no feminine sense.

Freda was too shrewd a woman to ignore the rivalry between Marcel and Grey, and if she intended to use it to her own personal advantage, she would have brought Marcel as her own partner.

'At least that's what I'd have done,' Kelly muttered half aloud, then grinned mischievously at the thought. She knew herself too well to really imagine such a ploy; she simply wasn't that devious a person. Which, she thought, was really too bad, because a more devious woman would make Freda's apparent blunder into her own advantage— if a blunder was what the gambit really turned out to be.

Kelly was far more inclined to think that Freda had invited Marcel as a gesture of . . . what? Contempt, perhaps. Something to show Kelly that Freda felt so secure about Grey's feelings that she could afford to be magnanimous and ensure Kelly's comfort during the party? Even that didn't make sense, but Kelly still didn't accept the simplicity of Marcel's explanations. There was something going on she didn't understand, and maybe she never would.

When Marcel returned with the drinks, she tossed hers back with unexpected relish and slipped another one immediately from the tray of a passing waiter. The move gained her an upraised eyebrow from her impromptu escort, but Marcel said nothing.

The alcohol combined with the unexpected turn of events and Kelly's own emotional turmoil to make her surprisingly lightheaded after a few more dances, and she had to retire to the powder room. There, a glance into the mirror revealed a Kelly she had seldom ever seen before.

Her critical if somewhat giddy appraisal revealed enormous brown eyes in a face flushed with excitement. The high-piled hair and the high neckline of the caftan top gave her an air of maturity and in the full-length mirror she could see that the rest of her outfit was equally complimentary. Where the black gown would have created a cheap, gauche impression, the rich colours and unusual style of the one she had chosen had turned her into a lovely and desirable young woman even by her own standards. Gone was the impression of a wild-haired teenager. She even looked taller!

Not that Grey was likely to notice, she thought. He hadn't yet put in an appearance, and she could only presume he was closeted with Sven Jorgensen over some business deal. The huge, bear-like host had also disappeared soon after Kelly's arrival, although she had noticed Freda circulating among the guests like a pale-haired Norse goddess.

Freda should have worn the black gown, Kelly thought. It would have suited her perfectly, perhaps even more so than the pale, icy-blue creation that graced the woman's astounding figure. In the blue dress Freda was the ice-maiden supreme; in the black she could have been queen of the witches—a role Kelly privately favoured.

When she returned to the party, Kelly's eyes automatically scanned the room for a sign of Grey, but he still seemed to be somewhere else, and she noticed with a tinge of antagonism that Freda, too, seemed to have disappeared. Marcel was speaking to her father in one corner, and Kelly drifted that way to join them.

A momentary lull in the music allowed her to shift quickly through the crowd, and she was nearly at her father's side when a huge paw closed around her wrist and the music frothed into a quick disco beat. Sven Jorgensen's voice boomed in her ear as the tall, bearded man avowed his intention to dance with her and quickly proved himself the equal of any younger man on the floor.

Almost any! During one swirling turn Kelly suddenly noticed a flash of unmistakable silver hair and her heart first leapt, then sank in despair as she saw the icy blue dress that flashed and merged against the dark handsomeness of Grey Scofield. He and Freda made an astonishingly handsome couple, she had to admit, while she and Freda's amazing father . . . ? 'It's like a grown man dancing with a child,' she breathed half aloud, suddenly angry with herself for making such an absurd comparison.

Certainly the size differential between herself and Sven, who must have been six foot six, was significant. But Kelly was no child, and she flashed a wild, vivid grin at her host as her feet lost their leadenness and carried her into the rhythm and tempo of the dance.

Sven Jorgensen gave a great whoop of enthusiasm as it ended, bowing outrageously to thank Kelly for her participation. Then he led her back to where Marcel and her father waited, pausing only to reach out one long arm and snare a jug of beer from a table.

'Hot work,' he roared, tipping up the beer jug and downing half its contents in what seemed to be a single gulp. Then he dropped a frothy kiss on Kelly's wrist and shambled his way off to seek another dancing partner.

'Isn't he amazing?' laughed Meg Scofield. 'A real modern Viking, and as genuine as anything. One day I fully expect him to swagger into one of his own parties wearing an iron helmet and waving a broad-axe in one hand and a joint of meat in the other. He'd drink all the beer, fight all the men and make love to all the women before throwing the prettiest one over his shoulder and vanishing into the night.'

'He's a little overpowering,' Kelly admitted, 'but I rather like him, actually.'

'Well, he sure likes you,' her father replied. 'He's already offered me four cows for you and says he'll raise the ante if you're interested.'

'Only four? *Tiens*! I myself will offer at least a dozen,' Marcel cried in mock seriousness. 'I will even throw in a few sheep and a moose for good measure.'

'Make it two moose and maybe we can deal,' Kelly's father replied with a grin. 'I'm rather partial to moose-meat.'

All of them were laughing at the suggestion when a gravelly voice from behind Kelly interrupted. 'I'd offer two moose just for a dance,' said Grey Scofield, but when Kelly turned to face him she found no laughter in his eyes. Instead, they flickered from herself to Marcel with evident hostility and she reacted without even thinking.

'I'm sorry, but I promised this one to Marcel,' she said coldly, and turned to find the tall French-Canadian thankfully ready to pick up her lead. They whirled away into the throng, but not before Kelly noticed the glowering chill in the gaze that followed them.

She would have shied then at the touch of Marcel's lips at her ear, but he held her so strongly in his arms that she couldn't move.

'Perfect! You have astounded me,' he breathed gently. Then he whirled her so that his apparent lovemaking couldn't be missed by any observer on Grey's side of the room.

'Do not shy away now. He is looking, I think. Oh yes, and if looks could kill I would be ten years already in the grave. Ah, Kelly, I did not realise you had the makings of such a vixen. You are truly the red fox,' he whispered, all the time nibbling at her ear as his arms held her close against him. 'Truly, you should have been a French-woman.'

He held her so close and kept them dancing in such a way that she couldn't possibly see what Grey's reaction might be and had to depend upon Marcel's vivid commentary. Nor could she free herself, which was mildly embarrassing because she could see the reactions of other dancers within her view and realised that to them it must appear as if Marcel was devouring her.

Finally, fortunately, the music stopped, and Marcel released her only enough to grin down with a lecherous smirk on his face. 'Exquisite,' he murmured. 'A classic performance. Come now, and we shall go and see if this Viking's food is as awful as his home.'

Kelly allowed herself meekly to be led away to the vast smorgasbord tables, which groaned with offerings of fish, fowl, meats and pastries and a host of foods she had never even imagined. She and Marcel toured the display like starving children in a candy store, trying a little of everything.

Kelly's professional eye was enthralled by the mixture of traditional Scandinavian smorgasbord and traditional Alberta home cooking. Like everything else about Sven Jorgensen and his home, the entire banquet was overdone, but it was done with a flair that she couldn't ignore, and she barely resisted the urge to sneak into the kitchen for a natter with the chef.

The music continued throughout their meal, and it was clear that guests were expected to eat, drink, dance or combine all three if it suited them. Kelly tasted only small portions of the seemingly hundreds of different dishes and sauces, but finally was forced to admit defeat.

At least, she thought, I've compensated for the drinks I've had. And she slipped across to the dessert table for just one final helping of an especially light Danish pastry, thankful she had never in her life been forced to think of dieting.

Throughout the meal, Marcel continued his outrageous flirting and gallant lovemaking, but as the rich, abundant food sated her lightheadedness, Kelly found his game increasingly made her ill at ease. She began to feel that everybody was watching them, yet when she looked around the crowded room there was no hint of such watchfulness. Was she imagining it? Or was Grey Scofield's intense interest sufficient to cut through a crowd of several hundred people? It would have been wonderful, she thought, to be able to believe he was all that interested. It was just too bad she couldn't share Marcel's oft-stated conviction that it was so.

She couldn't even spot Grey, neither among the brightly-attired dancers nor in the small crowds of people standing or sitting as they experimented with the glorious buffet offerings. She spotted her father and Meg Scofield in one corner, and her host in another with a fashionably-dressed, dark-haired woman perched upon his knees. But Grey and Freda were conspicuous by their absence, at least in Kelly's increasingly sober mind.

Finally she just had to get away by herself for a minute, and she excused herself to take a brief stroll through the huge, two-storied mansion. She said it was only to clear her head and try and shake down the enormous meal she had eaten, but in reality she just had to get away from Marcel's attentions, which had become increasingly cloying despite his good intentions.

She found, as the combination of alcohol and nerves was steadied by the abundant food, that she didn't want any more of this charade. What was possible between her and Grey, she was in no position to judge, but whatever it was or was not, there was no place for games like the one Marcel had begun. Grey could not, she felt, be influenced for the good by such a deception. Probably he couldn't be influenced at all, since his future seemed intricately bound up with Freda Jorgensen and her father.

Kelly strolled without thinking of what she saw, only vaguely aware of the enormous library through which she passed, of another room which contained only an enormous snooker table and accessories. From this, a door led to another, much smaller room, and as she entered it Kelly came face to face with Freda Jorgensen.

CHAPTER EIGHT

'You have . . . lost something, Miss . . . Barnes?' The blonde girl's icy exterior was mirrored in her deep blue eyes, eyes that roamed across Kelly's high-piled hair, taking in the enormous brown eyes, the dress and the figure beneath it with an almost masculine directness.

'I . . . I seem to have lost my bearings,' Kelly replied too quickly. 'I'm sorry if I disturbed you.'

'No.' The statement was accompanied by a small *moue* that revealed it to have been an automatic response. Freda was obviously thinking very quickly herself.

'You seem also to have lost your handsome Frenchman,' she said then, with just a trace of acid in her gentle voice.

'He is not *my* Frenchman, as I think you very well know,' Kelly replied calmly. The other girl's directness revealed an astonishing lack of subtlety, and perversely lessened Kelly's automatic fear of a confrontation.

Freda shrugged. 'As you wish. It is a pity for him, though. He has come a long way for your company.'

'And he shall go a longer one without it.' Kelly risked a blunt reply of her own, sensing somehow that this was not only a confrontation, but something far more elemental than that.

'That leaves you, then . . . alone.' There was a questioning element to the statement, but Kelly chose to ignore it.

'I've been alone before,' she replied with a shrug of her own.

Freda Jorgensen stepped back several paces, leaning one succulent hip against the large desk behind her. 'Loneliness is not such a good thing for a woman,' she said with a curious expression on her lovely, cool face. 'But then perhaps you have some other man already in mind.'

Again there was only the hint of questioning. Freda spoke with a calmness that was belied by the brittle quality in her eyes and a tenseness that Kelly could feel across the space between them. Kelly smiled to herself.

'There are many men in the world,' she replied with an unexpected chill in her voice. 'Are you thinking of someone in particular, Miss Jorgensen?'

Freda gave that curious little shrug once again, trying to portray a calmness Kelly knew the blonde beauty didn't feel. 'It is none of my business,' she replied. 'I have already the man who is important to me.'

Kelly thought of Grey Scofield, seeing in her mind again the strange dream she had had so soon after meeting him, and seeing with her eyes the attempt at confidence which the beautiful Freda couldn't quite bring off. Freda was frightened, and Kelly suddenly knew why. Freda was not at all confident of her ability to hold Grey, if indeed she even had him within holding distance in the first place. Brown eyes met chilled blue ones, but Kelly held her tongue, forcing the other woman to continue the strange, tension-fraught conversation.

'You know of course that Grey and my father are ... very close in business,' Freda said suddenly. 'That is why he was here early tonight, to discuss several very important projects of ... mutual ... benefit.'

There was a deliberate message there, but one which Freda was desperately trying to cover in cautious words. Kelly felt a sudden surge of something within her, some inner strength or weakness ... she didn't know quite what. But it told her that she, not Freda, was now in charge of this conversation.

'Not my business,' she responded calmly. 'I have my own business to run.'

'Your father's business. And when he takes in Marcel Leduc as a full partner? What place for you then?'

That statement was unexpected, and the question even worse. Was her father seriously considering Marcel as a partner? Worse, was he perhaps thinking of Kelly herself as more than just a business partner for the tall French-Canadian? Kelly shook her head in disbelief, unaware that it was a visible, physical gesture. No! Her father wasn't the type to consider things in such a light. But what about Sven Jorgensen? Could the huge oilman see business logic in an alliance between Grey Scofield and his daughter? Worse, would he go so far as to manipulate it?

'My father doesn't have to buy my men,' Kelly said flatly, and rejoiced at the flicker of cold blue eyes. That shot had struck home, and Kelly's stomach churned with the sudden realisation that she had struck a nerve in an almost mortal blow.

'I do not like your implication.' The blue eyes were angry now, but the anger wasn't enough to cover up the truth. And there was a haughty flash of something else in Freda's eyes . . . something akin to victory but not quite so blatant. Perhaps . . .

'Hasn't the deal been signed yet?' Kelly suddenly blazed forth, allowing her slow-building anger to rise in flames. 'Perhaps the price isn't high enough, Miss Jorgensen,' she snapped. 'Or perhaps there simply isn't a price high enough. It might surprise you that some men can't be bought.'

'He will be bought or he will be sold . . . broken.' The words came out in a furious, wolflike snarl, and Kelly saw again the fiery eyes of the blonde wolf of her dreams. Her stomach revolted in disgust and she bit on her tongue to keep from being sick. A part of her mind screamed at her to get out of this room, to find Grey and in some fashion warn him. Another cried equally loudly her faith in his character and his strength. But a third heralded the chilling truth. He *had* been bought; bought and paid for and wrapped up for delivery to this frozen ice-maiden with her beauty and her money and her father's power. Why else would Grey have spent half the evening closeted with his host, leaving his own guests early to come at the beck and call of a man whose power could buy his daughter anything?

Kelly fought back an inexplicable urge to reach out with her hands and close them around that slender ivory throat, to choke off the words even as they thundered into her brain.

'. . . He is mine!' The words echoed over and over as Kelly turned, fighting back the sickness as it rose to her throat, and stumbled through the door into the billiards room. From there she moved unsteadily back towards the brilliance of the main hall, seeing nothing and hearing nothing . . . only that hateful, triumphant voice.

As she reached the edge of the crowd, her vision swam back into a semblance of focus, but not enough to scan the milling throng and find her father. She must find him, she thought. Find him and somehow get herself away from this place. Away from the blonde she-wolf, away from this horrible, awful house, and most of all away from Grey Scofield and everything to do with him.

A touch at her arm brought her round in a fearful gesture that was only partially soothed by Marcel's soft accent. 'Come,' he said, sliding his arms around her and insinuating them into the slow-moving horde of dancers. Kelly wanted to resist, tried to resist, but could not. Marcel was safe, she thought, and she allowed her body to slump against him as the music soothed at the vibrant, ragged endings of her nerves.

He said nothing more as they danced, but used his body as a buffer to protect her from the touch of the other dancers, and his shoulder against her ear as a buffer against the harshness of the noise in the room. Kelly floated along with him, no longer totally in control of herself, no longer worried about her father, or about leaving the party. She didn't have to think, and so she did not.

The soothing of the music and the physical action of

following Marcel in the dance gradually brought her out of her mental confusion, and the slow, steady music helped her to regain a measure of composure. The music didn't stop, luckily, but slid from one slow number to another without allowing a pause.

'I think this dance is mine,' said a familiar voice at her shoulder, and as Marcel smoothly relinquished Kelly into her father's arms, it seemed as if he took her composure with him upon leaving the dance-floor.

'Oh . . . Dad . . .' she stammered, trying desperately to hold back the tears as her father gathered her close and let them spill on to his shoulder. She cried only briefly, taking refuge in her father's arms as she hadn't quite been able to do with Marcel, and gradually Geoff Barnes eased them off the dance floor and into a narrow, dim-lit hallway.

'It's Grey, isn't it?' he asked without preamble, and Kelly could only nod her assent. How he could make that assessment after taking her from Marcel's arms, she neither knew nor cared; all she required was his calming touch and his love and understanding.

'Do you want to talk about it?'

'Not here; not now,' she whispered. 'I just want to get away.'

'Right!' Geoff Barnes showed no sign of his earlier illness. Given the need, he was prepared to assume command despite the lines of tiredness on his face and the slow, painful movements he couldn't hide. 'I'll just say goodbye to our host.'

He left Kelly standing in the subdued light of the hallway, promising to return for her as soon as he had bade his farewells and given Meg Scofield some sort of explanation. Kelly seated herself on the edge of a low bench and wearily closed her eyes. Her father would handle what had to be done tonight, she thought, and tomorrow would have to be handled when it came. She closed her eyes and leaned back into the seat, only to rear forward with a start as her wrist was suddenly grasped in a strong yet gentle grip.

'I think we'd better have a bit of a chat,' growled the low voice of Grey Scofield, and without waiting for her assent he began leading her away down the hall.

Kelly yanked back against his grip, but it was if he was holding a frenzied horse. His fingers merely closed more tightly about her wrist and she was dragged along despite her protests.

'But . . . my father . . .' she began.

'He can wait. I want to talk to you now!' The voice was calm, yet alive with a tension that transmitted itself through his grip, and Kelly fell silent as he dragged her down the hall, around several corners and finally out through a narrow side door and into the garden.

In the pale moonlight, Grey's hair seemed to sparkle like fine silver wires, and his eyes shone out of a dark visage that was grim with determination and . . . anger? Or was it something else? Kelly couldn't tell in the dim light.

'Why have you been avoiding me all night?'

'I would have thought it was the other way round,' she countered in a low voice, hoping her emotions didn't show.

'I was tied up with business earlier on.' Grey stood like a statue, staring down at her. Then, almost absently, he released her wrist and reached into his pocket to extract a cigarette and his lighter. 'Do you want one?'

'No, thank you,' she replied grimly. 'I would prefer to just leave, if you don't mind.'

But she had waited too long. No longer occupied with lighting the cigarette, he was able to reach out and snare her wrist again just as she turned away.

'I'm glad to see you took my advice about the dress, anyway,' he said, and she fancied she saw the glimmer of a mocking grin.

'I took my own advice, thank you very much,' she snarled, struggling vainly to free her wrist. 'I don't need your advice on how to dress.'

'Could have fooled me.'

'It wouldn't be hard,' she snapped, and when she still couldn't free her wrist she turned to flail at him with her free hand, fingers distended like claws. To no avail; he merely reached up and caught that hand as well.

'Now that's more like the Kelly we all know and love,' he muttered. 'All fire and fury and ready to fight at the drop of a hat.' His harsh bark of laughter rang in her ears. Then, to Kelly's horror, his lips descended to touch ever so lightly upon her own. No harshness, no brutality, just a feather touch before he leaned away again and freed one of her hands so that he could bring the cigarette up to his lips once more.

She stood silent, watching as he breathed out the smoke in a ring that shimmered in the moonlight before it wisped away to nothing. Just like his feelings, she thought idly. But her lips burned as if that brief, ever-so-light kiss had been a brand.

'I'm still waiting,' he said quietly then.

'For what? Christmas?'

Grey smiled as he answered. 'For you to tell me why you deliberately snubbed me earlier on. And why you've been avoiding me. Is it because of the dress? Or because of the flower, which I must say looks very nice with it?'

Kelly felt her anger growing, and she shook her head and gritted her teeth. Reaching blindly upward, she scrabbled the silken flower out of her hair and flung it at him. It struck the shining whiteness of his shirt front and fell to the ground between them, lying like a dead bird in a little pool of light. Kelly stamped upon it, grinding the sole of her shoe down until the flower shape was gone.

'Is that your final word on the subject?' He was grinning again, that horrible, mocking, know-it-all grin that she found so infuriating.

'No,' she snapped. 'All I want is for you to let me go so that I can join my father and get out of this ... this mausoleum! So why don't you just let me go? We have nothing to say to each other.'

'I really get the feeling you're angry with me, but I can't for the life of me figure out why,' he replied softly. 'Don't you think I deserve an explanation?'

'Let's just say it's nothing I feel you could understand,' she replied.

'Your confidence is overwhelming. Why don't you try me?'

'Because I frankly don't care to, that's why. Now will you *please* let me go?' Kelly was squirming desperately now, but his grip upon her wrist, while not so tight as to be painful, was too firm for her to budge it.

'I'll let you go when I'm damn good and ready,' he snapped. 'Which won't be before you tell me what the hell's the matter. Even *you* couldn't get that upset about my objections to that black . . . black . . .'

'Black what? The only thing the matter with that black dress is in your own imagination.' Kelly had stopped fighting him, but her eyes blazed with growing anger, fanned by the fact she knew he was right about the dress and didn't dare admit it to him.

'It belongs in your trousseau, not at a party,' he growled. 'And what's more you know it, or else you'd have worn it tonight just to spite me. In fact, I'm damn well surprised you didn't, it's just your style.'

'*My* style? What the hell do you know about my style?' she retorted.

'I know what I like.' The statement emerged in a low, almost menacing tone. 'And that dress—on you—in public—isn't it.'

'Well, too bad,' she retorted. 'If I'd known it would upset you so much I'd have been sure to wear it.'

'I'm sure you would,' he snapped. 'So why didn't you?'

Kelly couldn't answer that question. It was too close to her heart. Breath coming in ragged gasps, she tugged once again against the grip at her wrist, but Grey was yet unwilling to let her go. Instead, he pulled her closer against him, flicking away the half-smoked cigarette as he wrapped his other arm behind her back and bent his lips to hers.

It took all her will power to let his warm, searching lips caress her, touching her lips with a gentleness that was totally at odds with the raging heat of their argument. She stood unmoving, neither resisting nor abetting him, until finally his lips moved away again and she could look up to meet his angry eyes.

'What was that supposed to prove?'

Grey shrugged, his lip curled in something between a sneer and a smile. 'Not a lot,' he said.

'Then why bother?'

'You still haven't answered my question about the dress.'

'Nor do I intend to,' she replied with a calmness she didn't feel. How dared he use his sexual charms in the middle of an argument? Didn't he realise the effect it was having on her? But then how could he? His affections were already bought and paid for.

'I prefer the one you're wearing,' he said then, with a softness she hadn't expected. 'At least under these circumstances.'

'Personally, I don't care which you prefer,' she answered.

'Like hell you don't!'

'Will you please let me go.' Kelly was fast losing her ability to argue with Grey. His very touch sent shivers down her spine, and she was beginning to fear that her body would betray her.

To her surprise, he released her hand without further argument. 'Have it your own way,' he shrugged. 'Lord knows why I bother with you in the first place—all we ever do is fight.'

'Which is hardly my fault,' she retorted. 'If you'd stop trying to run my life there'd be nothing to fight about, would there?'

She half turned to leave then, but his soft-spoken next words stopped her in her tracks. 'Has it occurred to you that if I didn't care about you I wouldn't bother?'

The reply emerged before Kelly could stop herself, and even though she regretted them instantly, the words continued to pour forth in a torrent she couldn't halt. 'Care? You don't care about anything but yourself and your precious camp,' she cried. 'Well, you can stop worrying about it now, because I've had it! Right up to *here*! With you . . . and your camp . . . and your . . . your *everything*! I'm leaving. Right now! So why don't you just go back to your little blonde girl-friend and her rich daddy. Maybe if you're nice he'll buy you a whole new camp, complete with cook!'

And before Grey could open his mouth, she had turned and was running away from him, running with tears streaming down her face, oblivious to the uneven paving of the path, oblivious of everything but her need to get away. She ran back through the doorway and down the crooked hall until she found herself sobbing in her surprised father's arms.

Geoff Barnes held her until the tears stopped, with Kelly's entire body tuned throughout for the footstep or voice that would warn her of Grey's return. But he didn't come, and finally she was able to raise her face and look her father in the eyes.

'I'd like to go now,' she whispered in a shaky voice.

During the ride back to the Scofield home, Kelly said nothing, her mind busy working out what she would do. It wasn't until her father had wheeled the station wagon into the drive that she spoke.

'Will you drive me to the airport if I pack quickly?'

'Of course, but . . .'

'No questions, please,' she pleaded. 'I just have to get away—now! I won't be going back to Kakwa; you'll have to send Marcel and I'll take his place if that's all right. I can work from home in Grande Prairie until we sort things out.'

'Kelly, are you sure you know . . . ?'

'I'm not sure of anything except that I have to get away

from all of this,' she replied, yanking open the door of the vehicle. 'Please, just bear with me.' And she ran into the house to pack.

It didn't take more than five minutes, minutes that stretched into hours as she threw things into her suitcases and quickly unpinned her fancy hairdo and tied her long hair into the more familiar ponytail. She left both the dress she had worn that night and the now-hateful black creation hanging in the closet and ran out to the vehicle, still expecting Grey to somehow stop her from leaving.

They drove in silence to the airport, only to find that Kelly couldn't get a flight north until early next morning. Wait? Not a chance, she thought. To wait would be fatal, giving Grey some further chance of catching up with her, if indeed he would bother.

'The bus station,' she decided out loud, forcing herself to ignore the look of patient resignation upon her father's long-suffering face.

'Kelly, I think you're wrong,' he said. 'Perhaps if I talked to Grey . . .'

'No! Oh, no,' she protested. 'Her heart sank at the thought of it. 'No. What's wrong between Grey and me is a personality clash, that's all it is. There isn't anything you can say to him, or anything you can do about it.'

'Oh, come on, child. I may be your father, but I'm not blind and stupid,' he replied almost angrily. 'You're in love with him; any fool can see that. But damn it, Kelly, even people in love have quarrels. Running away isn't going to solve anything at all.'

'If we were in love, I wouldn't be running away,' she cried angrily. 'But *we're* not in love. *I'm* in love. Which makes a great deal of difference, as you should very well know. Grey doesn't care a fig about me, or at least not enough to keep from taking on Sven Jorgensen's offer—daughter included.'

'What the hell are you talking about?' her father asked,

steering the station wagon into a parking lot at the bus station.

'I got it straight from the horse's mouth,' she replied with sudden bitter anger. 'Now please, let's not talk about it any more. It's over and done with. And not one word to Grey—I want your promise on that.'

'Whatever you say,' he replied grimly as he lifted her bags out of the vehicle and helped her carry them into the depot. 'But you're being a fool about this. Grey just isn't the type to . . .'

'Enough! Now kiss me goodbye and get yourself back to the party,' she said. 'I shall phone you from Grande Prairie to let you know I've got there safely. And please give my regards to . . . to Mrs Scofield and apologies for my strange behaviour, will you?'

Ten minutes later Kelly was on a northbound bus to Edmonton, seated alone with her thoughts on the seat directly behind the driver and feeling for all the world like a runaway child. Had she judged Grey too harshly? Was she being quite as ridiculous as her father had implied? Throughout the journey, on which the large motor coach barrelled up the freeway, she thought about the problem as clearly as she could. But it was no use, and by the time she reached Edmonton and changed buses, Kelly knew she had to live with her decision.

Right or wrong, it was at least a decision, and she knew it would be impossible for her to be as close to Grey as the confining circumstances of the camp required. Whether she was right about him having been bought, she no longer felt so sure, but she couldn't face the uncertainty and him as well.

She arrived in Grande Prairie long after sun-up but still before the city's business sector was more than half awake. And even that state was an improvement over Kelly herself. Lost as she was in thought, speculation and just a hint of self-recrimination, the lengthy bus journey had been a sort of waking nightmare for her.

The miles passed like the lights of oncoming traffic, remote, distant from the dreamlike state in which she travelled. She spoke to no one, and was not spoken to, although several young men passed approving glances at her trim figure and youthful loveliness. Unnoticed, at least by Kelly. It was like walking in a dream, walking without the need to wake, without the thought of waking.

Yet the trance-like state had not rested her, and once she had exchanged the bus for the less comfortable confines of a handy taxi and been driven to her father's house, exhaustion began to claim her.

Dumping her cases just inside the front door, Kelly moved through the house like a wraith, a part of her mind considering tea, another part breakfast, and the major part intent only upon sleep.

In the bathroom, hooded brown eyes stared out over dark, puffy areas of flesh. Even the eyes were dulled by pain, by emotional conflict, and by sheer sleepiness. She splashed cold water on to her face, wincing at its icy touch, but seconds later she was, if anything, even more sleepy.

Shambling, almost drunk with exhaustion, she closed the deadlocks on front and rear doors, then stripped away her clothing and stood, uncertain, her mind torn between shower and bed. The softness of the double bed with its eiderdown coverlet won easily.

She thought of a nightie, but the thought died before she really considered it. Lifting the coverlet, she slipped her slight, naked body beneath it, and was asleep virtually as her vivid hair struck the softness of the pillow.

It was a poor form of sleep, little better than her trance-like reverie on the bus, except that now her body could rest properly.

Not so her mind. On the bus, she had floated in a state that was neither sleep nor wakefulness, neither a true soul-searching nor a total escape from soul-searching. Here in a proper bed and with a feeling of security, her conscious mind gave her body the rest it denied itself.

She was mostly in that half-light drift that comes between wakefulness and sleep, a drift in which reality is bent
and exaggeration strengthened almost into truth. She knew
the physical sensations of Grey's touch, his kisses, the
strengths and muscles of his body. And she knew also the
responses of her own body, which shifted comfortably
under its coverlet as her nerves bent to the machinations of
her dreaming mind.

As the waves of pleasure pulsed through her, probing
and gently caressing her body like waves upon a beach, she
slowly drifted nearer to true sleep, the sleep of dreams and
. . . nightmares.

She was alone in a tall, murky forest, thick with dark
spruce and pines that muffled the sound of flowing water.
Alone, yet not really so. Around her were sounds of animal
movement, crashings of branches and crunchings of twigs.
There was no track, no obvious opening in the dank under-
growth, yet somehow she was in a clearing where no clearing had been.

And she was no longer alone; across from her loomed the
gigantic shape of a grizzly bear, a bear that walked like a
man and wore a man's clothing. Its teeth were pillars of
ivory, and they champed with a mushy, chomping sound
that drooled ropes of saliva down across a bushy, auburn
beard.

It lurched down upon all fours, stalking towards her,
and she could not move, could not scream. Only stand as if
all of her energy were drained, rooted to the ground like
the massive, watching trees around her. The animal's eyes
were piggy, pink with a raging fury that seemed to hyp-
notise her. Closer . . . closer . . . and one enormous paw was
outstretched, the talons alone larger than her fingers, far
larger than the bills that were stacked on its palm, held in
place by the claws.

The money stirred on the paw, banknotes now lifting

with a breeze that carried to her the bear's strong, cloying scent. She reached out, her fingers almost touching the money though she did not want it, fingers moving without commands from her numbed brain.

But a flicker of movement halted her, stopped her hand and caused the bear to shuffle backwards in a scurrying attempt to rise again upon its haunches.

The intruder was gaunt, moving with the lean, powerful loping stride of a hunting wolf. A grey wolf with startlingly grey eyes that shone silver as it turned to glare at her. And behind it, yet another wolf, only this one was a shimmering, almost metallic blonde colour.

The grey wolf held her in its gaze, eyes piercing like daggers of ice as it stared through her eyes and into her innermost, private self. But the pale wolf ignored her entirely, prancing lightly forward to gambol at the feet of the bear, leaping and twisting in a macabre dance.

Kelly could not twist away from the pale grey eyes, and her ears seemed stoppered. There was only silence around them, and the antics of the blonde she-wolf took on a demanding, pleading intensity. The form of it blurred, swirling like pale smoke as it spun more and more erect until its figure became horribly, beautifully, human and naked. But it had no face, only a yawning mouth filled with shining fangs and a pair of huge, ice-blue eyes that twinkled in the dim light.

Dainty hands plucked the banknotes from the bear's clumsy paws; slender, shapely legs carried the wolf-creature closer to allow taloned fingers to wave the money in the air, cutting the thread of staring between Kelly and the huge, gaunt grey wolf.

Only then could she focus properly on the sinewy blonde-crowned shape, and see with horror the hatred and insanity in its eyes. And she whimpered, and heard herself whimper.

The grey one snarled, and she heard that too, a snarl

that sounded like gravel rattling in a tin, rough and menacing. At the sound, the bear seemed to dissolve, melting down until only a misty paw remained to leave the money on the ground; then the animal was gone and only the wolves remained. Wolves? But yes, the female shape had shrunk away as the figure slumped lower, teeth bared in a snarl that encompassed not only the earth-bound Kelly but the other wolf as well.

The snarl was returned, and something—a flashing paw, a swift-moving muzzle?—scattered the paper money into a wind-driven miniature whirlwind that spun higher and higher until it disappeared above the swirling, mist-like figures. The blonde wolf leapt in, teeth bared and paws outstretched to reveal claws like those not of a wolf, but of a tiger. And where they touched, redness traced tiny lines across pale grey fur that slowly melted to reveal smooth, dark-tanned flesh.

Kelly screamed, and as she screamed she saw the blonde wolf-creature leap towards her, jaws champing as they flashed for a death-lock upon her throat. Again she screamed, twisting her body somehow so that the jaws clamped not on her vulnerable throat but on her shoulder, and as she did so the grey-wolf-man shouted her name, over and over again.

'Kelly! Kelly! Damn it, wake up!'

The sound penetrated, but not the words. And with the teeth grinding into her shoulder, Kelly screamed once more.

'Wake up!' The voice was more insistent; the jaws now shaking her entire body.

Her eyes fluttered open, and she would have screamed again had surprise not left her mute.

Grey took his hand from her shoulder, backing away from the bed with a strangely curious light in his eyes. 'My God, but you have vicious nightmares,' he muttered, turning to seat himself in a chair at the far corner of the room. 'Are you okay now? Awake, I mean?'

'Wh . . . what . . . are you doing here?' she managed to stammer, automatically reaching down to tug the coverlet up so that it covered her bared neck and shoulders. It was a ridiculous gesture of modesty, but made so without thinking that she had done it before the ludicrousness struck her. Then she frowned.

Grey still hadn't answered, but sat regarding her through half-closed eyes. An idle evaluation, it seemed, but his tenseness was revealed through the rigidity of his body and the taut cords of his neck.

'What are you *doing* here?' Her voice squeaked with the intensity of the question, and she struggled to raise herself in the bed without being too revealing about it.

'We haven't finished our little talk yet,' he shrugged, a hint of a grin playing about his strong, mobile mouth.

'Oh yes, we *have!*' The firmness she tried to inject into the reply didn't materialise, but he didn't appear to notice.

'Maybe you have; I haven't,' he countered. Then he leaned back in the chair, so that his dark green oilman's drill shirt strained across his wide chest.

He was too confident, too completely in control of the situation.

'I have nothing to say, and I'm not interested in talking to you,' Kelly said stoutly. 'Now please leave before I . . . I . . .'

'You . . . what?' There was a definite smirk there now, and Kelly felt herself growing tense with anger. The absolute nerve of the man, walking into her house, her bedroom, and demanding that she talk to him.

'I shall call the police,' she said defensively.

Grey crossed his forearms across that broad chest and showed his strong teeth in a downright mocking grin. 'Okay,' he said. 'Go ahead.'

She was halfway out of the bed without thinking, bare legs flashing from beneath the coverlet. Then, with a little shriek of comprehension, Kelly scrambled back beneath it and looked wildly around the room.

'My clothes! What have you done with my clothes?' she cried loudly. It was appallingly daunting to realise that she was there, naked beneath the coverlet, and that not only were her clothes gone from the bedside chair (or was he sitting on them?) but that the closet stood open—and empty. She couldn't possibly get out of the bed, much less call the police or anything else.

'You took my clothes,' she said, quite unnecessarily.

'Great powers of observation,' he replied mildly. 'Now about that little talk we were having . . .'

'How *dare* you?' Indignation raised her voice to a shrill squeal.

'It wasn't difficult at all, I assure you,' he grinned. 'And at least it will stop you from running out on me before we've finished . . .'

'We'll finish nothing,' she shouted, tears of anger starting from her dark eyes. 'I want my clothes!'

He grinned mockingly. 'Don't be any more naïve than you have to be, dearie. If you want your clothes you'll have to get out of that bed and find them, and you might as well understand right now that I'll have that quilt off you like the skin off a sausage before you reach the door. Not that,' and he paused with a grin that was positively wicked, 'I haven't seen you before in next to nothing. But then that was before I realised you are just about the most innocent, naïve, stubborn, pigheaded and downright stupid child in the entire world.'

'I am not!'

'Rubbish! And you're also pretty stupid if you'd let Freda Jorgensen run roughshod over you. What the hell did she tell you, anyway?'

Kelly snapped her mouth shut and glared at him. Games! He knew damned well what Freda had said; otherwise he'd never have brought it up. Well, if he thought *she* was going to further shame herself by repeating it for him, he had another think coming! Still, she couldn't help the flush that rose along the slender column of her throat, rising like a pink tide from the virginal whiteness of the coverlet.

'Or was it your pretty Frenchman who turned you against me so completely?' he continued, one eyebrow raised in a question that didn't hide the rigidity of his jaw.

He didn't know. He couldn't, or he wouldn't have brought that question up. He was only fishing, Kelly thought, and visibly relaxed with unexpected relief.

'Hah! So it was only Freda. I suppose I should have expected as much. All right, let's have it,' he demanded.

Kelly said nothing, her own jaw clamped in firm defiance. Until he reached over and tugged firmly at the bottom end of the coverlet. Then she shrieked.

'Stop that!' Both hands were clamped into a vice-grip on the top of the quilt, her legs flailing to keep beneath it as he twitched the bottom first to one side, then the other.

'Come on, talk, And hurry it up.'

Another twitch of the coverlet. 'All right,' she squealed. 'She . . . she . . . warned me off you, that's all.'

'Oh, did she?' He released the quilt and leaned back in that supercilious pose of commanding calm. 'And you, of course, said, "Yes, Freda; certainly, Freda," and then very daintily walked out to treat me like some kind of garbage. No way, sweetie. First, I can't imagine you being that easily dissuaded, and secondly it doesn't explain why I climbed so high, so quick, on your little blacklist. There's still plenty you're not telling me.'

'My *God*, but you're conceited!' Kelly countered, suddenly wild with anger. 'Yes, she warned me off you. Damned right she did. And I told her she was welcome to you, you . . . you . . . egotistical, chauvinistic pig. What do you think you are, God's gift to women? Just because some little blonde chippy thinks you're the greatest thing since sliced bread is no reason to think that I . . . I . . .'

'Oh, I don't know. I rather thought we had something

quite ... pleasant,' he replied. 'Apart from periodic attempts to poison me at the dinner table. Or am I to assume that you were just playing games—the kind of games you keep accusing me of?'

Kelly remained silent. Her anger made coherent speech nearly impossible, but worse was his apparent admission that he had really thought they ... she couldn't think about that.

'What else did she say to you ... I presume it was during the party?'

'You know. You must know, or you wouldn't be trying to do this to me,' she replied in a shaky voice.

'I don't, you know. Oh, I can guess. Freda and I are old ... friends, so I know the way she operates, but I don't know specifically what she said. And I damned well intend to know, or you're going to be in that bed a helluva long time.' Then he grinned that wolfish, mocking grin. 'So you'd better tell me before I decide I'm tired and come in there with you.'

'You ... you ...'

'Me ... me ... what? Hell, woman, what are you? Stupid as well as naïve?'

Then suddenly he clamped his mouth shut and stood up, walking over to stare down at her in a sudden, frightful silence. He stood there for what seemed like hours, his eyes boring into her. And when he finally spoke, it was through teeth that were clenched with anger.

'Damn you,' he murmured. 'I've never met anybody who could make me so angry I could strangle them without half trying. Now you're going to shut up and listen to me, because what I am going to say, I shall only say once. And by God, you'd better get it right the first time!

'I don't know what Freda baby said about me, and frankly I don't especially care. But I would have thought you knew me a bit better than to just sit there and swallow it, whatever it was. And don't bother to tell me it didn't matter to you anyway, because we both know better. You may not love me—lord knows you've tried hard enough to make sure of that—but you don't hate me either, no matter what you say. At least I would have thought you'd grant me the right of an explanation, though.'

And suddenly his hands were on her shoulders, dragging her up from the questionable protection of the coverlet. Kelly would have screamed, but his mouth was already claiming her lips, grinding against her in a kiss that was so angrily brutal it frightened her. She couldn't move, couldn't breathe, couldn't resist, until he released her mouth and flung her back against the bed with as much ferocity as he had lifted her away from it.

Then, to her utter surprise, he stalked to the door and flung it open. 'I'm going to make us some coffee,' he said in a grim voice. 'And we're going to drink that coffee, and then you're going to tell me what the hell is wrong, and you're going to listen to my explanation—if I have one—and then ... ah ...'

His final words were muffled, but the violence with which he slammed the bedroom door was sufficient to exhibit his anger.

Kelly lay back in stunned amazement. She had thought she had seen Grey angry before, but nothing like this. Now there was a barely-contained violence which both aroused and frightened her. She trembled, but it wasn't all fear. Just the touch of his hands, his lips, his anger ... she felt all quivery inside and was as frightened by the pleasantness of that feeling as much as anything else.

And what could she do? Clearly he was going to have his answers. With equal clarity, she had to admit he deserved them. But at what cost to herself? Did she dare to reveal her true feelings? Expose herself to ridicule, perhaps scorn? On the other hand, with the love for him she could no longer deny, could she continue to defy him? She thought about it, the words racing through her fevered mind as elusive as butterflies, and when he opened the door again she was ready . . . sort of.

At least he appeared somewhat more calm, she thought, striding smoothly into the room with a tea-tray heaped in coffee cups, sugar, cream and even biscuits.

He laid the tray across her lap almost gently, avoiding touching her as he did so. Then he dumped sugar and cream into his own cup, took it with a handful of biscuits, and retreated to his chair.

Kelly prepared her coffee, took a tentative sip and tried to hide an involuntary grimace at the strength of it. 'I . . .'

He waved a hand in a brusque gesture to cut her off. 'Drink your coffee first,' he said sternly.

'I'm *damned* if I will,' she snapped in sudden, unbidden anger. 'Just what the hell do you want anyway, Grey Scofield? First you come in here and threaten me because I won't tell you something, and then when I'm ready to tell you, you . . . you tell me to wait!'

'Patience,' he replied, 'is a virtue. And I have so few, according to some authorities, that it's one I try to cultivate. Drink your coffee.'

'I won't!' Kelly reached under the tray, only a heartbeat from throwing it at him, before she saw the glimmer of a smile as it wrinkled his lips. The devil! He was deliberately provoking her as usual, and as usual she was helping him. Well, not this time, Mr High and Mighty Scofield, she thought, and forced herself to relax and drink the bitter, scalding brew.

'You really make terrible coffee,' she said finally. It was an inane comment, but welcome in that it broke a silence that seemed ready to smother her.

'I know,' he grinned. 'Why do you think I hire people to cook in my camps? If I did the cooking I'd lose my men inside a week.'

Then he lapsed into a silence that was almost companionable, sipping at the horrible brew as if it was the elixir of life itself. And waiting. Kelly knew this was only a delay; the moment of reckoning would come.

'I can't finish this slop,' she said suddenly, shuddering at her final gulp of the brew. 'Are you ready to listen now, or is this some sort of third-degree torture?'

'I'm ready. But let me take that tray, just in case you decide to throw it at me again.' He grinned as he strode over to lift the tray, which he laid down beside the door. Kelly shot a tight grimace at him, both angered and somehow amused by his ability to read her mind, her every gesture. Why should she need to tell him anything, she wondered idly, when he seemed able to look into her eyes and knew it anyway? How could he possibly *not* know that she loved him?

'All right,' she said when he had seated himself, and then she told him exactly what Freda Jorgensen had said, omitting, of course, any hint of her own true feelings in the matter. Let him believe she had been merely shocked that he could sell himself in such a fashion. That was enough.

When she had finished, he laughed. And laughed . . . and laughed. Finally he said, 'Is that all? No engagement, no pregnancy, no half a dozen kiddies hidden away anywhere?'

'I should think you might take it a little more seriously than . . .' she began, but he interrupted her.

'And of course your only concern was my . . . principles?' he asked with that familiar mocking grin. 'You were merely offended at the suggestion that I could be so easily . . . bought?'

'Well, of course,' she replied, too quickly. He might not even have heard her.

'Your own feelings had nothing to do with it. All of this marvellous outrage, this absolutely splendid outrage—all for me and my so-called reputation, or character, or whatever you want to call it?'

'Yes.' She said yes, because what else could she say?

Even as the word emerged, it seemed hopelessly inadequate.

'Why?'

'What?' The question surprised her. Then it frightened her. What possible answer to that one?

'You heard me. Why?'

'Er . . . well . . .' Kelly stammered, playing for time, for anything! What could she say? Grey gave her no time, no chance.

'It wouldn't have anything at all to do with your own feelings? Not possible that you don't really hate me that much at all? No jealousy? No . . . love?'

The final words were a whisper that filled the room like a shout. Kelly closed her eyes, shivering with the tensions inside her. Of course I love you, you stupid man, she thought. But I shouldn't. I should hate you for torturing me like this.

CHAPTER NINE

SUDDENLY his fingers were on her shoulders again, but not harshly this time. Instead they traced the lines of her collarbone like fairy wings, meeting beneath her chin to lift it to meet his lips. Kelly kept her eyes closed, all her other senses being more than sufficient to gather in the touch of his lips as he kissed her so lightly, so gently, that she could barely feel it.

The light, fleeting touch went on and on, only his lips moving and the softness of his breath against her cheek like a warm breeze. His fingers stayed beneath her chin, still as any statue and yet warm, so incredibly warm.

There was no pressure, no force, no questioning, nor was it needed. Kelly slowly lifted her own arms to slide them around his neck, her fingers tangling in the short bristle of hair at the nape as she twisted her face to gather in his kiss.

Her mouth searched, trembling with the passion that flooded up from her thighs, bringing her breasts hard and firm as they lifted free of the cover. Her mouth flowered, softened, moulded itself to his.

Grey's fingers moved down, circling around her breasts with a touch that fired rockets in her brain and stirred a fiery warmth inside her. Then his lips followed them, searching down the line of her throat to capture each breast in turn. She reached up to capture his head, to hold him there for ever, but she could not.

The eyes that met hers when he lifted his head, straining against the pressure of her arms to do it, were a soft, dove-wing grey, textured like velvet with feelings she could no longer question. And his voice, too, had that velvet softness when he finally spoke.

'And to think I almost let you get away . . .'

Kelly was silent, her lips wanted kisses, not words, and her fingers tugged him toward her again.

'Oh-uh. We've got too much to do first,' he said hoarsely. And his huge, gentle hands lifted to press against her shoulders, holding her away from him as he straightened up and turned toward the doorway.

'Get dressed while you've still got the chance,' he said, his breath coming in ragged gasps. 'I'll be out on the porch.'

Kelly felt mildly ridiculous, scampering around the house naked in the five minutes it took her to find her clothes, decide they couldn't be worn again, and finally fumble her housecoat out of one suitcase. She looked at herself in the mirror, eyes no longer tired, but shining with an eternal glow from far within her, and found she couldn't be as generous about her hair.

'I'm going to have a shower first,' she said after opening the front door to find Grey sitting on the steps with a cigarette in his hand. 'I have time, haven't I? And to wash my hair and dry it? I can't go anywhere like this.' The words tumbled out in evidence of her excitement, and he smiled up at her.

'Depends how long you want to wait for your explanations,' he said. 'Or don't you reckon you need them any more?'

'I've got all I need,' she replied, meaning every word. His eyes raked over her, and she felt a shiver of . . . anticipation?

'I could do with a shower myself,' he said then, very slowly and deliberately. 'Shall I come and wash your back?'

'You shall not!' Kelly's outraged expression was a sham and they both knew it.

'Huh! I should have expected it, I suppose. It'll have to be marriage, eh? Won't settle for anything less?'

She paused before answering, choosing the few words with special care. There had been enough misunderstandings; this was no time for more.

'I'll settle for . . . whatever,' she said then, turning very slowly back into the house. She was halfway across the living room when a shrill whistle halted her in her tracks.

'You'll damned well wait for marriage,' said Grey when she turned around. 'Now hurry up and get clean, because we're flying to Calgary before this day is out and I hate flying in the dark.'

Grey staunchly refused to provide 'explanations' until they were airborne, although he was equally adamant that she must know the facts behind Freda's deceptive comments.

'I was selling out, actually, but not the way she said it,' he said. 'Her being part of the deal was just to get at you. You've met her father; you shouldn't have fallen for that part at all. He's as genuine a person as you'll ever want to meet.'

Annoyingly, he kept interspersing his explanations with tour guide directions through the windows of the aircraft, and Kelly thought she might never hear the full story before they reached Calgary. Grey insisted upon following the road south to Kakwa camp, waggling his wings as he did a slow loop around it and then circling the impressive Kakwa Falls twice to be sure she had a good view.

He's enjoying this, Kelly muttered silently to herself. And indeed he seemed to be, spinning the story out and making it sound even more dramatic than she had imagined from Freda's version.

'What I did do was sell out several of my holdings to Sven so that I could use the capital for something else,' he said.

And still later, 'She was half right about your father and the partnership, by the way.'

'Do you mean . . . Marcel . . . ?' Kelly was flabbergasted. 'Surely he wouldn't have done a thing like that without consulting me?'

'Certainly not if it was something exactly like that,' Grey replied with a shrug. 'But of course it wasn't *exactly* like that.'

'Oh, I do wish you'd just get on with the story and stop being obtuse and mysterious,' Kelly cried. 'You're starting to make me very angry.'

'Yeah, well, just don't start throwing things or anything. It isn't allowed in small planes,' he laughed. 'Okay, I'll tell you—partner.'

'You? I don't believe you,' she shouted. 'He wouldn't . . . he couldn't . . .'

'He did.' Grey uttered the words firmly, brooking no argument. 'Of course he didn't sell *you* out, just most of his share. You and I both end up with forty-nine per cent each and he's hanging on to the remaining two per cent himself—sort of a tie-breaker, he called it.'

'But . . . you can't even make coffee.' Kelly felt mildly hysterical. It was a dream, she felt, and yet it wasn't. She really was flying with Grey along the rugged flanks of the Rockies, and he really was telling her this.

And laughing. 'You'll have plenty of time to teach me before the children start arriving,' he chuckled. 'Although not too much time, I hope.'

'And what's that supposed to mean?'

'Well, your father hasn't anybody else to give him grandchildren, has he?'

'You two had it all worked out between you, didn't you?' Kelly asked, suddenly wary of this grey-haired, grey-eyed man she loved. 'What did he tell you, anyway?'

'Not one damned thing. In fact he refused to even talk about it. You should know your father better than that.'

'I'm not even sure I know myself any more,' she replied honestly. 'But then how did you know where to find me?'

'Easy. I read your mind. You should know that too, by now.'

'Too well. And I'm not sure I like it,' she replied. 'Am I really all that predictable?'

Grey laughed, an easy, comfortable laugh that restored Kelly's own good humour. 'You are the most unpredictable woman I've ever met,' he said then. 'I think that's what I love most about you.'

Kelly accepted that in the spirit in which it was intended; he had finally said he loved her, and nothing else could matter after that. They flew the rest of the journey in a gentle, euphoric silence, with Kelly napping part of the way and only coming fully awake when they swooped down upon Grey's private airstrip to find his mother and her father waiting for them.

Kelly was received with open, welcoming arms by both parents, each of them expressing in their own way a gladness and satisfaction that Kelly and Grey had finally worked things out.

She remonstrated mildly with her father about his re-organising of the business behind her back, but Geoff Barnes only laughed at his happy young daughter.

'Business before pleasure,' he chuckled. 'And now that the business is well and truly out of the way—when's the wedding?'

'Ask the mind-reader,' Kelly responded with a chuckle of her own, and Grey's response was expectably predictable.

'It'll be as soon as it can be arranged,' he said calmly.

And it was.

Apart from the families, only Sven Jorgensen attended the small, private wedding ceremony, and certainly the huge oilman's presence was less of a surprise than Grey's choice of a location for the service.

'It really is ridiculous to make me walk half a mile through the bush in a wedding dress and these impossible slippers,' Kelly told her father as the party negotiated the path to the crest of Kakwa Falls. She had found the unusual location difficult enough to imagine as they had flown down to the Kakwa in one of the huge Jorgensen helicopters, with Kelly in her flowing white dress and Grey looking resplendent in a morning suit.

But once on the ground, the spectacular venue proved a unanimous hit with everyone else, and Kelly had sufficient memories of her earlier visit to add to the new and even fonder ones she gathered on her wedding day.

There was still one more surprise, however, though it didn't eventuate until they were alone in their room at the exclusive Jasper Park Lodge.

The rest of the wedding party had remained for their own celebration after a splendid wedding supper of prime ribs of beef and Arctic char in the Moose's Nook.

Kelly emerged from the bathroom, suddenly and unaccountably shy as her wedding night began, only to find Grey had gone while she was washing, and left something vaguely familiar on the huge double bed in their room.

It wasn't the negligé that Kelly had left prepared for herself; indeed it was quite the opposite colour. And when she slipped through the darkened room and picked it up, she had to laugh out loud.

The infamous black dress carried a message all of its own, and it didn't really need the note that Grey had attached to it, reading: 'You can wear this now. Love, Grey.'

She chuckled as she slipped the gossamer fabric over her clean, cool skin, wondering at the logic of a man who would go to the trouble to keep such a troublesome garment.

And then she laughed aloud. She wouldn't be wearing it long anyway, she thought.

When Grey returned a few minutes later, carrying a magnum of champagne and a 'Do Not Disturb' sign for the door, she knew she was right.

Harlequin Plus

THE GIANT GRIZZLY

Try to imagine this scene: you're alone in the wilderness and suddenly you find yourself face to face with more than one thousand pounds of furred and ferocious animal. It rears nine feet in the air in front of you, swings its huge taloned paws and roars through slavering jaws....

A frightening vision? It should be! According to the native peoples of northern Canada, grizzly bears have been known to walk into an encampment and literally tear a man from limb to limb. It's said that these bears have been known to keep charging and attacking even when mortally wounded! No wonder, then, that grizzlies play a major role in the totems and legends of Canada's native peoples.

Some folks say that the name "grizzly" is derived from the grizzled appearance of the animal's brown coat; yet ask anyone who has observed a grizzly bear at close quarters, and he will tell you that the name is definitely descriptive of the fear this enormous beast inspires in its viewer's heart.

Grizzlies inhabit the northwestern Rockies of British Columbia and Alberta, Canada, and also wander the flat wastelands of the Arctic tundra. The land is harsh...and only the strong survive. And certainly the grizzly is a magnificent survivor!

4 FREE
Harlequin Romances